Death at the Dripping Tap

Veronica Vale Investigates – book 4

Kitty Kildare

Copyright © 2024 by Kitty Kildare

All rights reserved.

No part of this publication may be reproduced, distributed, or transmitted in any form or by any means, including photocopying, recording, or other electronic or mechanical methods, without the prior written permission of the publisher, except as permitted by U.S. copyright law. For permission requests, contact: kittykildare@kittykildare.com

The story, all names, characters, and incidents portrayed in this production are fictitious. No identification with actual persons (living or deceased), places, buildings, and products is intended or should be inferred.

DEATH AT THE DRIPPING TAP

ISBN: 978-1-915378-82-8

Book Cover by Victoria Cooper

Chapter 1

"Don't you know who I am?" I winced at the shrill panic in my tone and the entirely inappropriate question I'd blurted out.

"I know you've been nothing but a nuisance these past weeks." The trim middle-aged nurse, wearing a smart blue uniform, stood her ground, preventing me from getting farther into the hospital.

I drew in a breath, quelling my nerves. "I'm Jacob's wife! I have every right to see him."

The nurse didn't bat an eyelid at my bold lie. "He told me he's not married. Several of the nurses have been worried because he's had no one special visiting, so we enquired as to Mrs Templeton's whereabouts."

I ignored the heat rising up my cheeks at having been caught out. "The man has had a serious head injury. He's not thinking clearly. We're very close. We do everything together. We're as good as married."

"Inspector Templeton wasn't wearing a wedding ring when he came in. I should know, since I removed his personal items."

I blinked back a sudden rush of tears. I'd been coming to the hospital daily since Inspector Templeton had almost lost his life during an explosion at a slum clearance. Occasionally, a kindly nurse let me in for a brief visit, but most of them prevented me from seeing him. It was family only or police officers who were permitted entry. Which was why I'd resorted to desperate measures, pretending to be Mrs Templeton to get access to his room.

"Veronica! There you are." My best friend and ever-loyal supporter, Ruby Smythe, hurried along the corridor, her coat and hat in a complimentary shade of green. "I've been walking around this hospital for ten minutes. I didn't know Jacob had been moved."

"He's out of danger, and we needed the bed for somebody else in the acute wing," the nurse said.

"Why couldn't you have told me that?" I snapped. "When I found the bed empty, I thought the worst. I thought..." Tears threatened again, and I gulped them back. I'd never experienced such a tremulous hold on my emotions.

"You shouldn't have been able to see his room," the nurse said. "I don't know how many times I've had to remind you, but he needs rest. Being bothered every day will only set him back."

"Surely, he welcomes the company," Ruby said brightly. "And it would save you a job, so you wouldn't have to look in on him while we're here."

"No unauthorised visitors. And the last time I checked, he was asleep. That's an end to this conversation. You should go home. It's getting late and visiting hours will be over in half an hour."

Ruby held out a brown paper bag. "Can I tempt you with grapes? They were ever so expensive. They're for

Jacob, but you do such good work here, I'm sure you'd enjoy them."

"It'll take more than grapes to bribe me. Go home." The nurse turned and strode back to her station, keeping her beady eye on us so we'd be unable to slip past and get to Inspector Templeton.

"You look exhausted." Ruby gently tugged me over to a seating area. "Have a rest. Eat a grape."

My stomach grumbled with hunger, but I had no appetite. I'd barely eaten since the dreadful news reached me about Inspector Templeton.

Ruby popped a grape into my mouth, despite my protest that I didn't want it. "I picked up a copy of the evening edition. They're still running stories about the explosion. We're all mentioned again. Especially our hero, Benji."

I closed my eyes. "I don't need a newspaper to tell me my dog is perfection."

She flapped open the broadsheet. "Here it is. 'Hope was fading as desperate volunteers, policemen, and firefighters dug through the rubble to find those caught in the recent explosion on Barton Avenue. There were calls to end the search for fear of another undiscovered bomb or a gas leak setting off an explosion, but the fearless team continued on. The hero of the night was a fearless hound called Benji, who belongs to local reporter, Veronica Vale. The plucky dog dug for hours before unearthing a faint cry for help. It was Inspector Jacob Templeton, a decorated former soldier and experienced police inspector, who was dug out of the rubble. There is talk of giving the hero dog a medal.'"

"Benji would be quite content with a bag of bones," I murmured. "They need to stop raking over the ashes. We all know what happened. So many bombs were dropped on London during the Great War that it's a miracle this doesn't happen more frequently."

"Everyone loves a happy ending." Ruby's gaze flicked across the page. "And from the sounds of it, things are looking up for Inspector Templeton. Since they've moved him onto a regular ward, that must mean he's on the mend."

"I need to see him to be certain of that," I said. "But that stubborn nurse refuses to let me pass. I even told her we were married."

Ruby burst into laughter. "Imagine that! No one would ever be able to convince you to walk down the aisle. I hope I was your bridesmaid at this imaginary wedding."

"Of course." I delicately sniffed and took another grape. "And the right man would tempt me, but you know I'm content with my situation."

Ruby squeezed my elbow. "Your situation is one few women would consider, though. We've been born into lives where it's expected for us to marry, look after a home, and raise a family. You're breaking the mould. But that doesn't mean you don't deserve happiness, too."

"When have I ever said I was unhappy?" I asked.

"You haven't smiled since Jacob was brought in here," Ruby said. "I know you pretend to dislike each other, but you almost lost him. It's shaken you. Maybe even changed your mind about a thing or two."

I pressed my lips together. My relationship with Inspector Templeton was not as straightforward as I'd assumed. We enjoyed antagonising each other, proving

DEATH AT THE DRIPPING TAP 5

each other wrong, and occasionally working together to solve a crime. It had never crossed my mind that he may disappear from my life. So when I'd received the terrifying news of the explosion on the night he was supposed to take me to the Policeman's Ball, everything had shifted off its comfortable axis.

And in the small hours of the night, when I was in my bed alone, I'd got to thinking. What if I liked Inspector Templeton more than I realised? What did that mean? Could we ever be more than friendly antagonists to each other?

Ruby pinched my arm.

I jerked away. "What was that for?"

"I was checking you weren't asleep with your eyes open. You'd gone quiet."

"I was in my thoughts. If I was able to see Inspector Templeton, I'd be more settled."

"Is it not busy at the newspaper?" Ruby asked. "Can't Harry keep you on your toes and your mind on other things?"

"Now the worst of the winter cold is over, there are fewer deaths to report on. I still have obituaries to write, but Uncle Harry is going easy on me, given what's happened to Inspector Templeton. He keeps asking how I am and awkwardly patting my shoulder. I'd rather he treated me the same as always."

"He's trying to help," Ruby said. "Didn't he say he'd drop by one evening and see how things are? I know he's friendly with Jacob."

"Hopefully, Uncle Harry will be by tonight," I said. "And he let me leave work an hour early so I could avoid the traffic." I was determined to keep my routine ordinary, despite the extraordinary circumstances I found myself in. I was still going through the motions of sleeping, dressing, and heading into work, but it was an illusion. My thoughts were on one thing. No matter how hard I tried, I could barely focus on anything else.

"Did you stop in at the house on your way here?" I asked.

"I did." Ruby glanced at me. "Your mother looked pale and said her stomach ached. Benji won't leave her side. He seems concerned about her well-being."

Neither Matthew nor my mother had been themselves since the news about Inspector Templeton reached them. "My mother is excessively fond of Inspector Templeton."

Ruby nodded. "And I suppose, given everything Matthew went through during the war, it must have shaken loose bad memories."

"Matthew almost keeled over when he learned the extent of Inspector Templeton's injuries."

"He wasn't the only one," Ruby said. "There we were, in our best dresses, ready to be entertained and dance all night, and this terrible business was flung at us."

I grimaced at the painfully fresh memory. It felt like we were living in a nightmare. We were putting on brave faces, but the cracks were showing. Even Ruby looked rumpled, and she always took the greatest care of her appearance. But she was juggling her work, helping with my family, and supporting me at the hospital whenever she got the chance.

"There's Sergeant Matthers!" Ruby said. "He'll have news. Good news. Mark my words."

I stood as Inspector Templeton's right-hand man, Sergeant Matthers, strode towards us. He nodded a greeting as he took off his helmet, revealing sparse, dark hair. "Do you two have beds here? Whenever I arrive, you're already settled in for the evening."

"I won't go until I get an update," I said. "But it appears I'm forbidden from seeing Inspector Templeton."

Sergeant Matthers glanced away. "Don't take it personally. He's not keen on company. I even got told to shove off the other day."

I stood, my brow furrowing. "Has he been telling the nurses not to let me in?"

Sergeant Matthers still wouldn't meet my gaze. "It's his injuries, you see. He's all bruised and bashed about."

"I couldn't give two hoots about his appearance," I said. "I need to know how he's faring. And I'm sure an interesting conversation over a cup of strong tea would do him good. Can't you get the man to see sense?"

Sergeant Matthers raked a hand through his hair. "I shouldn't tell you this, but the last meeting with the doctor didn't bring the news he was hoping for. They're concerned about the leg injury."

I swallowed the lump forming in my throat and lifted my chin. "The nurse who refused to let me in said they'd moved him out of acute care because he was doing so well."

"He is! And the doctor was happy with his progress. But it's the leg, you see. It took the brunt of the explosion."

Ruby stood and gripped my arm. "Jacob will pull through and be on his feet in no time, scolding Veronica for interfering in his investigations and pretending he doesn't find us useful."

I blinked away tears. "I'm sure he will."

"There's nothing wrong with his brain," Sergeant Matthers said, his hangdog expression brightening. "He's even insisting on working. I brought in some files. Just cold cases, but I thought they'd keep him busy. Might make him cheerier to look at old photographs of murders."

"You see!" Ruby said. "You can't keep a good man down. While he's in here, he'll solve a dozen cases, and most likely receive a promotion. He'll have his own station to run by the time this is over."

I sniffed back the wretched tears. It would do no good to have a red nose and swollen eyes when I finally got in to see Inspector Templeton. "Sergeant Matthers, could you put in a good word for us with the nurse? We only want five minutes, and then we'll leave."

Sergeant Matthers's gaze turned apologetic. "They're strict and always do what's best for the patient. And if the patient says he doesn't want visitors other than those connected to his work, they'll make sure he's not bothered."

I resisted the urge to stamp my foot. I was so irrationally angry, a swell of unsettling waves constantly lurching in my stomach. "We do work together! Or has he conveniently forgotten how many cases we've assisted with?"

"I'll talk to him," Sergeant Matthers said hurriedly. "I've got to go. I'm still on duty, so I'm not supposed to be here, but I promised I'd drop these files off. I'll get into

DEATH AT THE DRIPPING TAP   9

trouble if the chief discovers what I'm up to, sneaking case files out of the station, but I know they'll help."

"You're looking after a valuable colleague," I said. "You can't get into trouble for that."

Sergeant Matthers mumbled that he hoped that was true, checked with the nurse at the station, and headed along the corridor. I made a careful note of which room he entered, so I knew where to go when the opportunity arose. And it would. I was getting in to see Inspector Templeton.

"Try not to worry about the leg injury," Ruby said. "If the worst happens, he'll still be capable. We saw men injured during the war get on with their lives. Some even work!"

"His career means everything to him. I don't know what he'll do if he doesn't have that job. It's his life."

"An officer that valuable won't be discarded," Ruby said. "They look after their own."

"There you are!" Uncle Harry walked along the corridor wearing his usual outfit of dark suit trousers, a shirt with the top button open, and his tie flipped over one shoulder. "I've been sent to three different wards in my search for Jacob. How's he doing?"

"I've been unable to visit him," I said. "Apparently, Inspector Templeton only wants visits from people he works with. The nurses aren't letting me in."

Uncle Harry glanced at the nurse station. "I know her. We ran a story about a local blood drive, and she was in charge. I interviewed her. Let's see if my old charm works. While I keep her busy, you can sneak in."

I hugged Uncle Harry. "You're a lifesaver."

He chuckled. "If it gets the sad look off your face, I'm happy to charm anyone. Give me a few minutes, then off you go."

While Uncle Harry distracted the nurse, Ruby fussed with my hair and attempted to smear lipstick on me.

I gently pushed away her hand. "There's no need for that."

"There's every need. You need to look presentable for your inspector. You don't want him to think you're unnecessarily worrying about him, do you?"

I bit my lip as she finger-combed my hair. That was something that scared me much more than Inspector Templeton's slow healing injuries. Maybe I did want him to know I was worried.

Chapter 2

I'd never tiptoed so fast in my life, Ruby beside me as we dashed to Inspector Templeton's room. Uncle Harry had handily manoeuvred the nurse so her back was to the corridor we scurried along. Whatever charming things he was saying worked. The nurse was giggling like a schoolgirl on her first date.

I stopped, my hand on the door that would reveal Inspector Templeton to me.

"You can do this," Ruby whispered. "You saw him the other week when he was barely conscious and you came out the other side. The fact he's been moved here will only mean an improvement."

I drew back my shoulders, ignored the rapid tap-tap-tap of my heart, and entered the room. I barely noticed the neat furnishings and bunch of flowers on a small side table. My attention was taken by the grumpy, bandaged man in the bed.

Inspector Templeton's dark eyes narrowed when he saw me. "I said no visitors."

"Untrue. You're being selective about who visits. I know Sergeant Matthers is around here somewhere." I strode into the room, pretending this was just another day, and I was doing nothing as extraordinary as visiting a man who'd been at death's door only a few weeks ago.

"Sergeant Matthers is here for work reasons. You're here to cause trouble."

"When I go anywhere, I'm only being helpful," I said.

Inspector Templeton lifted a hand to touch the dressing on the side of his head, partially concealing a deep gash and a swollen eye.

"You look divine." Ruby set the grapes down. "Almost back to normal."

Inspector Templeton tutted. "It's clear you've received no medical training, if that's what you believe."

"I got the basics during the war. That knowledge got me through with barely a scratch." Ruby peered at Inspector Templeton's covered legs. "I hear everything is healing nicely."

"It doesn't feel like anything is healing. Everything hurts, so the last thing I need to add to my list of troubles is a blinding headache because I won't be left alone to sleep."

I ignored the slight and walked to the other side of the bed, so Inspector Templeton was cocooned in our steely affection. "You must be bored on your own. What do you do all day?"

"Recover from almost being blown up. That takes energy and silence."

"I got a nurse to rustle up some tea for us." Sergeant Matthers appeared in the door with two cups and saucers in his hands. "Oh! You got in."

"They're not staying," Inspector Templeton said. "And they're only here to cause a nuisance. I expect Miss Vale wants to write an article about me."

DEATH AT THE DRIPPING TAP 13

"You are yesterday's news. Last week's, in fact," I said.

"There is an article in the evening edition," Ruby said. "You were mentioned again. You're a local star."

Sergeant Matthers set down a cup of tea near Inspector Templeton. "One good thing that's come out of this mess is they've put a stop to the slum clearance. It's too dangerous to risk any more men out there."

"It's a pity such a terrible accident had to happen before they came to their senses," I said.

Inspector Templeton grunted a reply.

"Have the doctors said when they'll discharge you?" Ruby asked after a few seconds of awkward silence, only Sergeant Matthers slurping and blowing on his tea, breaking the silence.

"No one is saying anything helpful. They don't know what they're doing," Inspector Templeton said. "And they insist I take pills that knock me out."

"That'll be for the pain relief," I said. "You must be grateful for that."

"I'll be grateful when people leave me alone and stop giving unwanted opinions. That includes you."

I took a step back, his words stinging. "There's no need to be unkind."

"And there's no need to make a fuss and keep sneaking in here," Inspector Templeton said. "None of you. I know what you've been saying to the nurses to wheedle your way in."

"I can't imagine what you're referring to." I neatened the flowers in the vase.

"Why do you keep telling them we're married? They know it's untrue."

"Because you had the sense knocked out of you and are refusing to see me," I said. "What did you expect me to do?"

"Respect my wishes. I don't want anyone seeing me like this."

I held in a sigh of frustration. "I'm not just anyone."

"You're a perpetual thorn in my side. Wherever I turn, there you are, with your sharp tongue and unhelpful comments."

"Steady on," Sergeant Matthers said.

"It's a pity I wasn't there during the slum clearance to keep an eye on things." I fixed Inspector Templeton with an icy stare that masked the stab of pain in my stomach. "If I had been in that building, I wouldn't have made the error of blundering about and activating an unexploded bomb."

"This is my fault?" Inspector Templeton gestured at his legs.

"I'm not saying that. But you don't have to be so unpleasant. We're here to help."

"You always say you're helping, yet you never do."

"Need I remind you of the cases we've helped you solve?" My insides trembled. Inspector Templeton had never spoken to me so rudely before.

"I was capable of solving those cases, but you never allowed me the opportunity to," Inspector Templeton said. "You interfere where you're not wanted. Just as you're doing now."

"Jacob, we're friends," Ruby said. "Of course, we want to be here to help with your recovery."

"It's Inspector Templeton to you! And we're not friends," he retorted. "I put up with your meddling because I have no choice. It's less trouble to entertain your nonsense suggestions and poking around than to have you arrested on trumped-up charges. I'm not quite that cruel, but I have been tempted."

"Now you're just talking drivel," I said. "Are you sure the doctor thoroughly examined your head wound? It seems the little sense you had has shaken itself loose."

"We should take a break," Ruby said. "Get a cup of tea and let the gentlemen talk."

"We're going nowhere. It was almost impossible to get in," I said.

"Then you wasted your time," Inspector Templeton said. "I don't want you here."

My temper flared, heating the back of my eyes. "Do you think I want to be in a hospital at this time of night?"

"I don't know what you want," Inspector Templeton said. "You owe me nothing. I'm not one of your unwanted dogs abandoned at a shelter to take pity on."

"I know that! And as Ruby said, as much as you don't want to admit it, we have a friendship of sorts. If the situation were reversed, you'd visit me, and I'd welcome it."

"You wouldn't. You're prouder than I am. You'd want no one to see you in this situation." Inspector Templeton gestured at the door. "Sergeant Matthers, make them leave."

He shuffled from foot to foot, not seeming to know what to do, his anxious gaze darting between us and the cup in his trembling hand.

There was a tap on the door, and I tensed, concerned it might be a nurse.

Detective Chief Inspector Taylor entered the room. He stopped short when he saw us. "Blimey. You're a popular chap. Sergeant Matthers, should you be here?"

Sergeant Matthers set down his cup. "I was just taking five minutes and wanted to see how things were going."

"Of course. You're a good fellow, but the world doesn't stop because one of our finest is out of action." Detective Chief Inspector Taylor strode over, his broad shoulders and confident air filling the room. "Feeling better yet, old man?"

"Almost as good as new." Inspector Templeton forced a grimacing smile.

"Excellent. I want you back on the team as soon as possible. I expect to see a quick recovery." Detective Chief Inspector Taylor was brashly confident, and knew his position, uniform, and aquiline nose appealed to many. Unfortunately, when you scratched the appealing surface, there was little useful substance beneath.

"I was talking to the doctor this morning, and we're already discussing a discharge date." Inspector Templeton glanced at me, a warning in his eyes not to contradict him.

"That's even better news. Some rest, exercise, and you'll be fine. And there are plenty of men who have had worse injuries and they've made full recoveries. Besides, it'll be quicker to get you back on your feet than to train someone who's wet behind the ears. Isn't that right?"

"I couldn't agree more, sir," Inspector Templeton said.

Detective Chief Inspector Taylor turned his attention to Ruby, a slick smile spreading across his face. "My dear Miss Smythe, I didn't realise you two were such good friends. Or do you always visit men down on their luck?

Like a hard-luck story, I suppose. Some ladies do. The lost lamb effect."

Ruby didn't return his smile. "I consider Inspector Templeton an excellent chap. I greatly admire him. Even though he doesn't like to admit it, I consider him a friend."

Inspector Templeton spluttered a few words.

Detective Chief Inspector Taylor attempted a smoldering look, making him appear constipated. "If only we all had friends as lovely as you. Let me tempt you to dinner one evening. If you grow faint around a man in uniform, you'll be proud to be on my arm."

How inappropriate! But how like Detective Chief Inspector Taylor to think only of himself in a situation such as this. I'd always thought little of him. He drank too much, made inappropriate advances towards Ruby, and cared more about his reputation than the well-being of his officers and the community they served.

"My diary is fully booked," Ruby said.

"Come now, you must have one evening free," Detective Chief Inspector Taylor said. "I'll take you to the best places. We'll have fun."

"I'm too busy to think about fun," Ruby said. "And you must be shorthanded at the station. Inspector Templeton wasn't the only officer injured during the explosion, was he?"

Detective Chief Inspector Taylor's nostrils flared. "There were a few other injuries. One of the men is already back at work. Solid chap. Can always be depended upon."

"I'll be back as soon as I can." Inspector Templeton attempted to sit straight, but his wince suggested it hurt too much to achieve success.

"Excellent!" Detective Chief Inspector Taylor looked at Sergeant Matthers. "We won't take up anymore of the ladies time. I'll see you back at your desk soon, Templeton."

Sergeant Matthers inclined his head, gesturing so Inspector Templeton knew where the cold case files had been hidden. With a hasty goodbye, the two men left.

I turned to Inspector Templeton. "You lied to your superior! Your injuries are serious, and they'll take months to recover from. You can't go back to work until you're healed."

"You don't know anything about my injuries. You're not a nurse," Inspector Templeton said. "You need to stop interfering."

"I may not be medically trained, but I saw enough war wounds to know you may lose that leg."

Inspector Templeton sucked in a breath, small dots of colour flaring on his pale cheeks. "You've not seen my records, and you've not inspected my leg. Nor will you. I'll heal from this, and I'll be fine."

"You should have let Detective Chief Inspector Taylor know how much time you'll need to recover," Ruby said softly. "The way you were talking, he's expecting you back in the office any day."

"That's where I intend to be as soon as possible. They can't keep me here, so once they've done everything they can for me, I'll discharge myself and get on with things."

"Don't be ridiculous. Who will look after you when you leave the hospital?" I asked. "Since you so bluntly stated you weren't married, you don't have anyone to care for you."

"I'll manage. If necessary, I'll employ a home help."

"Veronica has room in her family's home," Ruby said. "You could move into a spare bedroom, just like I did when recovering from being poisoned."

Inspector Templeton scowled at me. "I couldn't think of a worse nursemaid."

"Nor I a worse patient," I spat back.

We glared at each other, neither wanting to budge. My heart felt bruised by his cold indifference. While my logical side realised Inspector Templeton felt embarrassed at being in such a weakened state, the rest of me wanted to comfort him. He had tough times ahead, and I needed him to know he wasn't alone.

"Why don't you look at the files Sergeant Matthers brought you?" Ruby crouched and pulled out three plain files full of papers. "He said he's got cold cases you'll be interested in. It would be a feather in your cap if you solved them while you were on your sickbed."

Inspector Templeton barely spared the files a glance. "I told him to find me some fresh cases. What's the point of bringing me cases that I have no chance of solving? It's not as if I can head into town and make enquiries."

"He was being helpful," I said. "You should be more grateful."

Inspector Templeton speared me with a fierce glare. "Why are you here? I can say without a shadow of a doubt, we aren't friends. We tolerate each other, and that's an end to it. I need neither of you here. Go and don't come back."

"You silly old thing. It's only the pain medication making you talk like that." Ruby gripped my elbow, aware how much his words hurt me. "Perhaps we'll give you a day or two off and try again. And you must eat the grapes I brought you. They'll cheer your mood."

Inspector Templeton waved away the words and the fruit. "I'm done. Nurse! There are intruders in my room. I want them to leave."

This time, I didn't bother to hide my anger as rapid footsteps approached the door, and the stern-faced nurse appeared.

"How did you get in here?" she asked. "I won't have people bothering my patients. Don't make me bar you from this hospital."

"Please do," Inspector Templeton said. "I'll get no rest until they're prevented from visiting."

I didn't bother with a goodbye. It would only be tossed back in my face. I stomped out of the hospital with a quiet Ruby beside me. My hands were in fists, and my breath came too fast. The man was a stubborn-headed buffoon. His pride was getting in the way and stopping him from seeing sense. We hadn't visited to poke fun, get a story, or belittle him. He needed help. And I wanted to support him.

"Jacob didn't mean anything he said." Ruby stood with me outside the hospital in the cool evening air as I worked through my feelings. "He's on a lot of medication, and he's humiliated. The finest of men would say the most foolish of things in those troubling circumstances."

I nodded, not speaking for fear my voice would wobble.

"Jacob will apologise when he's had time to stew and realise his error," Ruby said. "He was foolish and stubborn, and he will regret it."

"He's both of those things," I said. "We've done nothing wrong."

"I agree with that." Ruby paused. "But you're as bad as each other."

"What do you mean?"

"You're two peas in a pod. A perfect match, except neither of you realise it. Both too stubborn and too foolish to admit how fond you are of each other until a crisis hits. Now you've locked horns and refuse to give way. What kind of outcome can you expect from that behaviour?"

I closed my eyes and massaged my forehead. I really had no idea.

Chapter 3

Even though I was working on a fascinating obituary involving a wealthy aristocrat, an overweight goose, and an icy cold pond, I struggled to concentrate on the details. It was Inspector Templeton's fault. Why couldn't the man see sense and accept my assistance? Was he really so stubborn headed that he refused to comprehend he'd been beaten by a bomb? Was there nothing I could do to make him see how reckless he was being by attempting his recovery alone and forcing an early return to work?

I shook my head and hovered a pencil over my notepad, waiting for inspiration to strike. I should follow Inspector Templeton around more closely to ensure he did nothing so foolish again. Did he not have the sense he was born with? Surely, the bomb couldn't have been so small as to be missed. What did he do? Kick it to see if it started ticking like a misbehaving schoolboy?

Benji gently whined as he rested his head on my knee. He'd been a never-ending source of comfort since I'd almost lost Inspector 'Stubborn-Headed, Won't-Listen-to-Reason' Templeton. Benji only left my side when he couldn't accompany me to the hospital.

"We'll make him see sense. Inspector Templeton may think he's independent, but he needs us." I looked at Benji and drew in a breath. "Perhaps he needs you! Or a version of you. A support dog. A well-trained dog to help him get around until he's back on his feet. Of course, if he only has one foot to stand on, he'll need even more support, but we'll tackle that tricky business when it's upon us."

Benji gently thumped his tail on the floor.

"Yes! It's an excellent idea. I'll finish here, and we'll go to the dogs' home. It's unlikely our rescues will be suitable for such a task, but we have connections everywhere. I just need to find a way to convince Inspector Templeton this is the perfect solution." I ruffled Benji's fur. "If he ever gets in trouble again, he'll have a four-legged companion to ensure he escapes in one piece. And just think, if he'd had a dog with him when searching the slums, it would have detected the unexploded bomb and herded him from danger."

The trickle of uncomfortable tension that kept every muscle in my body tight eased. Even if I couldn't find Inspector Templeton the perfect support dog, going to the dogs' home would give me a purpose. I could focus on the animals, who always accepted my help. Unlike a certain stubborn-headed hospital patient who was preventing me from writing suitably soothing words about a dead man and a goose.

Progress made, I was able to get my head down.

Someone raspily cleared their throat too close to my desk. I glanced up and repressed a grimace. Bob Flanders lurked close by, his trousers unpleasantly crumpled at the crotch and what appeared to be a brown stain on his green shirt. Perhaps a dollop of sauce had fallen out of his breakfast roll. He had a liking for greasy fried egg sandwiches.

I stared at him, and he stared back. I wasn't intending to break the uncomfortable silence. If he wanted something from me, he'd have to jolly well ask.

He cleared his throat again, which turned into a coughing fit that grew so intense I almost thumped the sickly fellow on the back before he fractured a rib.

"If you're quite done with dying, I have work to focus upon," I said.

Bob's choking subsided, and he patted his chest with the flat of his hand. "I know you're having a tough time."

My spine stiffened, and my eyes narrowed. "From the sticky rasp in your throat, you're the one in trouble. It's all the cigars."

"I smoke a pipe!"

"Even worse. The smell always lingers."

Bob's jowly scowl surfaced before vanishing. "That fella you're always hanging about with, the inspector. Everyone knows what happened to him."

A tight band of tension wrapped around me. "What does that have to do with you?"

Bob shrugged, struggling to look me in the eye. "We don't get along, but it's a tragedy when someone you're close to is hurt."

I tilted my head. "Are you speaking from experience?"

"My younger brother, Wilfrid, he got called in to serve in the last year of the Great War. We thought he'd got away with it, given his health was never on par, but as the men fell, the standards lowered, and he got drafted."

"I didn't know you had a brother," I said. "Did Wilfred make it back?"

"Most of him did. But there were parts left behind. They never returned." Bob hoisted his trousers, then tapped the side of his head. "No one can figure out how to fix him. He got caught in an explosion, just like the inspector, and he took a bad knock. He's not been the same since."

"That's a tragic story, but I don't understand why you're telling it to me." I didn't mean to be harsh, but I wasn't in the mood for sharing sad stories with Bob. I didn't trust or like the man.

"All I mean is ... if you need a break, I've spoken to the other men. We'll take over your workload. Write the obituaries so you can focus on helping. There's nothing worse than being stuck in a hospital bed with only the walls for company."

I pretended to drop my pencil to give myself a few seconds to hide the shock. Bob had never been kind to me. He was an active tyrant, always trying to turn people against me and convince Uncle Harry I wasn't fit for purpose.

"I don't expect you to take up the offer," Bob said. "After all, when Harry sees what an incredible job other people do, writing those obituaries, he'll have no reason to keep you around."

I glared at him, but it softened when I saw the expression on his face. He wanted to help. For the first time in living memory, I'd discovered Bob's softer side. It made me immensely uncomfortable.

"While I appreciate the gesture, I find keeping busy useful. There's little I can do to help Inspector Templeton while he's in the hospital."

Bob nodded slowly. "We're lucky no one died. The coppers had cleared out all the homeless and were searching the last rooms when Inspector Templeton stumbled across that bomb."

"The slums are dangerous places," I said.

"There's a team being put together to search the remaining buildings to make sure there are no more bombs," Bob said. "It's not unusual to find a cluster together. German pilots would offload on their way home, so the planes weren't so heavy and they wouldn't run out of fuel. Could be there was a dodgy batch that fell in the same area."

I shuddered. "Perish the thought of anyone else being hurt."

"I'm following the team. Writing an article about their mission," Bob said, a hint of pride in his voice.

"You've been tasked with such a daring endeavour?" I failed to hide my surprise.

"Harry picked the best man for the job. It was only natural he'd come to me."

I arched an eyebrow.

Bob chuckled, which turned into another cough. "Maybe not physically, but I'm a whiz at what I do. So much so, I could easily take on your job too and not break a sweat. There's nothing to scribbling a few words about a dead person. I expect the relatives tell you everything, anyway. You're really nothing more than a nosy shorthand assistant."

Benji growled softly.

"While your offer is appreciated, you should leave while you're ahead," I said.

Bob reached out a hand as if to touch me, swiftly withdrawing it when Benji growled another warning. "I should get on."

I watched Bob walk away, feeling lightheaded. Since I'd just witnessed a miracle and discovered kindness hidden within the most acerbic character, it gave me hope that anything was possible, even Inspector Templeton's swift recovery.

I blinked away tiredness and stifled a yawn behind my hand. I'd barely been sleeping, what with one thing and another. It didn't help that Matthew and my mother's health sat on a tremulous knife edge. Matthew had barely got two words out since he'd learned about Inspector Templeton's injuries. He'd hidden in his room for two days, and I could hear his night terrors were back. If only I could convince him to visit Inspector Templeton, he could see for himself how he was doing. It was so easy for one's imagination to run to the worst scenario when you didn't see the facts for yourself.

After I'd collected a strong cup of tea and two plain digestive biscuits from the tea lady's trolley, I had the energy to finish my obituary. Words written, I was considering a short lunch break when Uncle Harry called me into his office. I collected my notepad and pencil and hurried in, with Benji by my side.

"Shut the door, Veronica," he said.

I did as instructed and sank into the chair in front of his desk. As usual, the desk was littered with editorials to be checked and letters to be dealt with by his secretary.

"How are you doing, old thing?" he asked.

"Please, don't be nice to me," I said. "Anymore kindness and I will cry for the rest of the day."

His compassionate smile almost tipped me over the edge. "Chin up. It's a tough time, but Inspector Templeton is made of stern stuff."

I sniffed back tears. "Did you get in to see him at the hospital yesterday after we were escorted out?"

"I got a couple of minutes. But my charm only stretched so far, and the nurse got wise I was distracting her so you could get in. She wasn't happy about it, but I got her free tickets to the ballet on Maiden Lane. That mollified her somewhat."

"I appreciated the help." I resisted the urge to chew on the end of my pencil. "What did you think when you saw him?"

Uncle Harry pressed his lips together. "He's doing a good job of hiding the pain. What I gathered from the nurse was that his injuries are still considered serious."

I failed to stop a tear from falling and quickly swept it away.

"She was optimistic, though," Uncle Harry said speedily. "Providing there are no complications with the leg, he should be out in two weeks. Maybe less."

"That's good. I talked to him about getting support once he's been discharged from the hospital," I said.

Uncle Harry grimaced. "I can imagine how that conversation went."

I thumped my hand on the chair's arm. "He's such a proud man. How is he expected to look after himself while recovering from such injuries? And you should have heard him downplaying things to Detective Chief Inspector Taylor."

Uncle Harry regarded me levelly. "Did you offer to look after him?"

"No! Although Ruby suggested he move in."

"With you and the rest of the family?"

"It's ridiculous, I know. I thought it a ludicrous idea." I hesitated and dropped my gaze. "We do have the room, though."

"It's inappropriate," Uncle Harry said. "I'm not entirely sure what your relationship is—"

"It's a friendship. Nothing more. Sometimes, not even that."

"Whatever it is, is it your place to take on another walking wounded?" Uncle Harry's tone was gentle. "You watch over Matthew and Edith. You volunteer your time at the dogs' home. And you like to help out now and again when the police have a murder investigation they're struggling with. Isn't that enough?"

"I do those things willingly." I sank against the seat as another wave of tiredness beat against my weary brain. "Inspector Templeton has little family, and I don't want his health to suffer when he leaves the hospital."

"I could have a word with him, talk practicalities. Keep the emotion out of it."

"I always have an excellent handle on my emotions." I dabbed away another irritating tear.

"Most of the time, you do. But this isn't a typical day. It's not been a typical few weeks." Uncle Harry passed me a clean white handkerchief. "With you rallying for that fine fellow, he'll have no choice but to make a full recovery."

"I told you not to be nice."

"I'm being truthful. You'll terrify him into getting better."

"That's what I intend to make happen," I said. "I was considering finding him a support dog. The Vet Corps has placed dogs with former soldiers who need support. It's an informal arrangement, but it makes the world of difference. Maybe there's a dog out there for Inspector Templeton."

Uncle Harry considered the possibility. "If anyone can make it happen, you can. I suppose you could loan him Benji."

Benji lifted his head and wagged his tail.

"They get along famously, but I couldn't be without Benji," I said.

"Suggest it and see what Inspector Templeton thinks. You don't want to add to his burdens, though. If having a dog around causes an inconvenience, it could be more trouble than it's worth."

"Dogs are never a trouble," I said. "And I could walk the animal. Benji is friendly to all, so that won't be a problem."

"And it would give you a reason to stop by and check on how Inspector Templeton's recovery was going, wouldn't it?"

"The thought never crossed my mind." I gave Uncle Harry a small smile. "I was about to get some lunch. Would you like anything?"

"Don't go just yet. I didn't call you in here to talk about Inspector Templeton."

"Do you have a new obituary for me?" I asked. "I've just finished with the overweight goose."

"In a way. I've heard of some trouble at the Dripping Tap."

"The pub on Newchurch Lane? It can be a rough area. Stanley's not been injured, has he?" Stanley Pickleton had managed the Dripping Tap for almost a year. He was one of my pricklier landlord's, not liking a woman as his employer, but not brave enough to suggest I give up work, put on an apron, and serve my husband his favourite pie and mash dinner.

Uncle Harry sighed. "I'm sorry to say Stanley's been arrested for murder."

Chapter 4

The shocking news made my maudlin concerns vanish. "Murder! Do you know the details? Who was the victim? Where did it happen? Why do the police think Stanley was involved?"

Uncle Harry shook his head. "I could only get basic information from my contact at the police station. They're still in disarray after the explosion, so everyone is pulling double shifts and battling exhaustion. I got a name, though. Arthur Blackstone. Apparently, he was found outside the Dripping Tap."

"Why do the police think Stanley killed this man?" One hand gripped the edge of the chair, the other rested on Benji's head as I absorbed this terrible news.

"That's all the detail I have, other than that Arthur's body was covered in dirt and some kind of white wool. I'll keep digging, but I thought you'd want to know."

"If the police think Stanley was involved, there must have been an eyewitness," I said. "Who could it be? A customer in the pub?"

"I tried for more information, but I drew blanks."

"When was he discovered?"

DEATH AT THE DRIPPING TAP 33

"In the early hours of this morning. That's as precise as I could winkle out."

"An eyewitness account so late at night won't be credible. Who would be out at such an hour and what sort of condition would they be in? If they'd been in the pub all evening, they'd be three sheets to the wind," I said. "This death may have no connection to the Dripping Tap or Stanley at all. It was just unfortunate the attack happened outside the pub and an inebriated chap got the wrong end of the stick."

"We should be grateful Arthur wasn't found inside the pub. Any more bodies on the premises, and you'd get a reputation," Uncle Harry said.

"My mother has made me acutely aware of that problem," I said. "This must be a mistake. Stanley can be difficult to handle, but I've never seen him become violent."

Uncle Harry sat forward in his seat. "I wouldn't be so sure of his innocence. When a job takes me to that side of town, I sometimes drink at the Dripping Tap. Especially when it's cold. Stanley always has the fire roaring. When I've been there, I've seen things that made me wonder about him."

"What kind of things?"

"I saw him lift a man off his feet and throw him out the door. He's got a short fuse, and he's strong. Add in alcohol, and we have trouble on our hands."

"No, surely not. I got the measure of his character when I interviewed him for the position," I said. "I'll admit, Stanley has rough edges, but he's an experienced publican. You don't thrive in this business if you intimidate your customers, and the Dripping Tap turns over a healthy profit."

"My contact seemed certain Stanley was involved. And I trust the fellow to tell the truth. Stanley, I'm not so certain about."

I shook my head. "I'll tell the police they've made a mistake. I can provide a character reference for Stanley and clear this up. Besides, as soon as he supplies an alibi, this nonsense will be over."

"Veronica, if you poke about in this murder, tread carefully," Uncle Harry cautioned. "You don't have Inspector Templeton on your side."

I arched an eyebrow. "I never have him on my side. He's usually behind me, shoving me out of the way."

"Don't be obtuse. You know what I mean. He lets you get involved, but another inspector won't be so obliging. You could find yourself in trouble."

"I can assure you, Inspector Templeton does his utmost to make sure I don't help, despite how useful I can be," I said.

Uncle Harry huffed out a laugh. "Maybe so, but don't think you can walk into any old crime scene and get your way."

I accepted the challenge with a determined nod. "Perhaps it won't be such a simple matter, but I'm not giving up on Stanley. He deserves better. And if he has a temper, we don't want him losing it and causing any more trouble for himself."

Uncle Harry sighed. "I was in two minds about telling you because I knew you'd do this, but you're right. You need to make sure he's treated fairly. Take the afternoon off and sort out this situation."

I jumped from my seat, kissed Uncle Harry on the cheek, and assured him I'd be careful. I swiftly collected my coat and handbag, and was out the door with Benji beside me two minutes later.

It was a busy lunchtime, and although the going would be slow in a taxi, if we went to the pub on foot, it would take at least an hour.

The Dripping Tap was located in the East End of London, an area yet to see significant regeneration following the war. If Inspector Templeton considered the slums a problem in this part of the city, he'd be horrified by the situation in the parish I was about to visit.

I hailed a taxi and climbed inside with Benji, giving the cabbie directions. I hadn't visited the Dripping Tap in over a month. I had a timetable of visits scheduled to ensure the pubs were properly maintained and the landlords had no concerns. Unfortunately, the last time I'd visited the Dripping Tap, it had been closed because of a burst pipe. Stanley had failed to inform me of the situation, which I'd been less than pleased about.

We were still working on how to communicate. He didn't appreciate a woman's interference, as he called it. Even though that woman was his employer, who paid his wage. It had caused us to spar a time or two, but when I inspected the books, I was happy to see a tidy profit. Stanley may not like me, but he ran a successful enterprise.

The journey across London was slow, the traffic building up, and the sound of horns honking and people shouting making it a less than pleasant trip. Normally, I'd take the hustle and bustle in my stride, but my nerves had felt frayed ever since Inspector Templeton ended up in hospital. I'd never considered myself fragile, but every person had a breaking point. Was I reaching mine?

Eventually, we pulled up outside the Dripping Tap. I paid the cabbie and climbed out with Benji. I wasn't surprised to see the doors to the pub shut and two police officers standing outside, preventing anybody from getting in.

I smoothed the front of my skirt and strode over to them, Benji close to my heel. An unfamiliar-faced officer of no more than twenty-five held up a hand as I approached. "Sorry, miss, the pub is closed due to an incident."

"I'm aware. I'm the owner. Veronica Vale. Could you tell me what's going on?"

The officer glanced at his companion. "That's all the information we can share with members of the public."

"I'm not a member of the public. I understand the landlord, Stanley Pickleton, has been arrested for a possible murder. The victim was assaulted outside the pub. Is that correct?"

"I really couldn't say, miss," the officer said. "You need to move along."

I crossed my arms over my chest. "I'm going nowhere until I have answers. Who's in charge?"

"Detective Chief Inspector Taylor," the other officer said. "And he's busy inside."

It would do me no good to argue or attempt to barge past these officers. They were only doing their jobs, and doing them most effectively, much to my frustration. "I'll wait for him out here. Perhaps you would be so good as to tell him I'd like a moment of his time."

After they'd stared at me for several seconds in silence, the first officer disappeared inside the pub. He returned a moment later. "He'll be out soon."

With Benji in tow, I walked past a row of small shopfronts selling everything from loose tobacco to toiletries. The road had an air of faded hope lingering in the buildings crumbling cracks. There were several empty spaces, most likely shops that took a hit during the war and had been cleared away rather than rebuilt. It would take more than a shake and a fresh lick of paint to regenerate this area.

I was beginning my fourth circuit when Detective Chief Inspector Taylor finally appeared. He talked to one of the men at the door as I hurried towards him.

"Detective Chief Inspector, I must speak to you," I said.

He ignored me for several seconds, still talking to his officer, before finally turning my way. "Miss Vale! There was no need for you to visit. We have everything under control."

"I'm not sure you do. I need to know why you arrested my landlord for this murder."

He caught hold of my elbow and guided me away from the pub. "Don't think about such unpleasant business. We're here, and we will sort everything out."

"The business may be unpleasant, but it is mine." I extracted my elbow from his grip. "I need to know what's going on."

"Are you worried the business will suffer? You shouldn't think about such trifles." His gaze ran over me. "I'm amazed your father left you in control of such an unfeminine enterprise."

"The lack of femininity is neither here nor there. He picked the best person for the job."

"Whatever you say, my dear." Detective Chief Inspector Taylor's tone was laced with condescension. "No Ruby with you? You girls are joined at the hip most of the time."

"Ruby is working," I said.

"She needs a suitable chap. Then she can give up all that nonsense. She does something with horses, doesn't she?"

"Ruby is an experienced equestrian. Shouldn't she put her talents to good use?"

He smirked. "As pretty as she is, she's not getting any younger. Put in a good word for me and convince her to accompany me on an evening out. I have access to all the best spots. She'd want for nothing."

"Shouldn't you focus on this investigation, and not escorting my best friend on an evening soiree?"

"I'm capable of both."

"If that's the case, then give me the details. I need to know what happened."

His expression hardened. "There's nothing for you to know. I don't know how you found out about this, but I won't have you interfering."

"I have every right to be here. You've closed one of my pubs and arrested my landlord. And I'm not convinced you've done it for the right reasons."

"Why else would I arrest a man if he wasn't guilty of a crime?" Detective Chief Inspector Taylor asked.

"You've arrested Stanley because he's an easy target," I said. "Take this investigation seriously. Don't pick on somebody vulnerable because they fit your assumptions."

Detective Chief Inspector Taylor stepped into my personal space, ignoring Benji's growl. "Be careful how you speak to me. I will not be humiliated in front of my men. I know you take liberties with Inspector Templeton, but he's not here. You won't flutter your eyelashes and get your way with me. Now, if you'd brought Ruby along, things would be different."

The man was the very definition of an unprofessional imbecile. All he cared about was closing cases quickly and having an attractive woman on his arm. He was more interested in maintaining his facade of excellence rather than ensuring justice was done. It rankled every nerve in my body, and I found myself clenching my fists and having to hide them behind my back.

"We've got off on the wrong foot." I drew in a calming breath. "I only want the basic facts."

"You have them. Someone was murdered outside of your pub, and we have the man who did it."

"Has Stanley confessed to the wrongdoing?"

"It's only a matter of time before we get the information from him."

"Can you talk me through what happened? What leads you to believe Stanley is guilty of such a dreadful crime?"

"Twenty years' experience working on the police force has given me an instinct to know when a man is guilty. Stanley was unhelpful when we spoke to him. He also lives above the pub, so it would have been easy for him to attack the victim and sneak away to tidy himself up."

"How did Arthur die?"

Detective Chief Inspector Taylor jerked back. "What do you know about the victim?"

I winced. My tiredness and anger had got the better of me, and I'd revealed details I shouldn't know. "You told me his name."

"I did no such thing. I know you're a reporter, so you have your sources, but don't expect them to be reliable. We're not releasing information about the victim or the manner of death until we're ready to do so."

If only I had Ruby's ability to charm and flatter even the most odious of men, but it was beyond me. "I'm not here to cause trouble, but I do need to know what happened."

"And in good time, when I see fit, you will do so. Good afternoon, Miss Vale." Detective Chief Inspector Taylor turned and strode back inside the pub, the determined slam of the door a sign I should not follow.

I glowered at the door. That man was three times as stubborn as Inspector Templeton and half as intelligent. Instead of wasting any more time, I found a taxi and instructed the driver to take me to the police station. I strode inside and up to the desk, where a perky-looking female police officer sat. It was rare to see a woman on the desk, so I was hopeful I'd get sense out of her.

"May I help?" she asked.

"I'm here to visit Stanley Pickleton. He's being held for questioning over the unfortunate situation at the Dripping Tap. I'm his employer, Veronica Vale."

"Let me see what I can do." She made a few telephone calls and came back to me. "Sorry, he's being processed and interviewed. He can't have visitors."

"What about legal representation?" I asked.

"I thought you said he worked for you."

"Yes! He does, but I may want to represent him, too." I gave her my most imploring look. "Please, I'm worried about him, and I need to make sure he's not in any trouble."

"Miss, he's on a murder charge. It's about as much trouble as you can get into. I am sorry, you won't be able to see him. At least not today. Maybe when he's been charged, there'll be time for visitors."

I repressed a groan. Everywhere I turned, I was being defeated. I hurried out of the police station to the telephone box at the end of the road. I called Ruby's place of work, and after a moment, an exacting butler brought her to the telephone.

"Veronica! Is there a problem?" Ruby sounded out of breath.

"Yes, and I need your help to fix things."

"Is it Inspector Templeton? He's not taken a turn for the worse, has he?"

"No, as far as I know, he's still rallying," I said. "But you must join me at the hospital after work. I'm in need of a distraction."

Chapter 5

"You look too glamourous to be unwell." I stood beside Ruby outside of the hospital, a crisp evening breeze ruffling my hair.

"I can fake a faint with the best of them," Ruby said. "My mother has been saying recently she's been getting an attack of the vapours. I'm unsure what it means, but she gets red in the face and overheats. She often has to sit and loosen her clothing until she's cooled down. I'll behave like her. I'll even throw in a swoon for good measure. That should cause a suitable distraction so you can talk to Inspector Templeton without the nurses bothering you."

"I just need five minutes with him. He should know more about the goings-on at the Dripping Tap. The pub's reputation will be known to the police." I sighed. "I should have paid more attention, then Stanley wouldn't be in such a bother."

"That is a seedy part of London," Ruby said. "I don't blame you for not wanting to visit more frequently. The Dripping Tap doesn't have the charm of some of your other pubs. The few times I've been there and asked for a dry martini, Stanley laughed at me. And the last time I visited with you, he served me half a Guinness and said it was full of iron."

"I suspect there's little call for martini around those parts. I'll have a word once he's out of trouble."

"Did Stanley ever mention having a problem with this Arthur chap?" Ruby asked.

"If he was having any trouble, he'd have kept it to himself," I said. "Whenever we communicate, it's only one-word replies from him. Stanley feels uncomfortable having a female as his employer."

"He needs to get used to it, or move on," Ruby said. "Shall we get this over with? It looks like the shift is changing, so the new nurse may not recognise us. She'll also be busy checking her paperwork and the patients to worry about two harmless souls visiting a dear friend on his road to recovery."

I caught hold of the door as it opened, and a gaggle of nurses hurried out, chatting to each other. I deliberately turned away because I recognised the strict nurse who'd prevented me from getting in to see Inspector Templeton.

Once they were gone, we rushed inside and walked along several corridors until we came to the wing where Inspector Templeton was recovering.

"I recognise the nurse on the desk," I whispered to Ruby. "She didn't let me in the last time I asked."

"Then it's time to ensure all eyes are on me, just as they always should be. You take cover, and I'll get the vapours forming." Ruby's eyes glittered with excitement as I tucked myself around the corner so I could see when the coast was clear.

Ruby did a sterling job of staggering from side to side. Unfortunately, she looked less like a woman having an attack of the vapours and more like someone who'd had half a dozen extra dry martinis on an empty stomach. She almost crashed into a medicine cart, avoiding it at the last second as she weaved towards the startled-looking nurse standing behind her station.

"Miss, are you quite well?" the nurse asked.

"I feel ever so hot. My vision is blurry and my heart is racing."

The nurse was instantly by her side, and Ruby was quick to shuffle around, so they had their backs to me. It was the best opportunity I'd get, so I snuck out and hurried past, not looking back, and hoping the nurse kept her attention on Ruby and didn't see me slipping into Inspector Templeton's room.

I eased the door shut quietly. Inspector Templeton was in bed, his eyes closed. Despite his injuries and bandages, he was a handsome man. If he wasn't so stubborn, he'd have found himself a suitable lady. He never talked about his private life, though, so I suspected he didn't have one. Some men were married to their jobs.

I wondered what they did when they no longer had those jobs? Most likely, they withered and died like an unattended orchid in a cold room. I didn't want that for Inspector Templeton. For all his stubborn-headed refusal to see my value most of the time, he deserved kindness. We all did.

"Veronica, are you going to stand there all evening staring at me, or have you come to ask a question?" Inspector Templeton's voice was soft in the still room.

"How did you know it was me?"

"I recognise your scent."

I pushed away from the door and walked towards his bed. "Excuse me?"

"It's the perfume you use."

"I rarely wear perfume. Only for special occasions. Perhaps you mean my hand cream." I thrust one hand under his nose.

"That would be it. Some sort of flower?" He opened his eyes, his level stare causing my heart to skip.

"Roses. I wouldn't bother with it, but my mother buys me lavish sets of cosmetics and ladies' pampering lotions every Christmas. I don't want to hurt her feelings by not using it."

"What are you doing sneaking in here?" he asked. "You're banned from the hospital."

"You didn't mean that." I tugged on the edge of the bedsheet to straighten it.

"Don't fuss. I have to deal with the nurses coming in, checking, taking my temperature, sticking me with needles, giving me pills to send me to sleep. I just want to be left alone."

"If they did, you'd stew in your misery, and that would make you absolutely no fun." I walked around to the other side of the bed and discovered a box of unopened chocolates. My stomach made a most unladylike growl.

"Help yourself," Inspector Templeton said.

"I didn't come here to eat your gifts." I gently shook the box. "Where did these come from?"

"There was a collection at the station. Sergeant Matthers brought them in. I told him to leave them with the nurses, but he said they preferred tins of biscuits."

"Perhaps I'll have one." I opened the box, looked through the descriptions of the chocolates, and chose a caramel cream. "You have one, too."

"The drugs make me feel sick," Inspector Templeton said. "Veronica, what are you doing here?"

I took another chocolate and popped it into my mouth, giving myself time to gather my thoughts. It had taken a certain amount of pride-swallowing to visit. I hated to admit how much I relied upon Inspector Templeton to get a foot in the door when there was an unsolved murder to investigate.

"Your silence speaks volumes," he said. "What's going on inside that head of yours?"

"There's been a spot of trouble at a pub," I said. "The Dripping Tap over on Newchurch Lane."

"The East End? That's on the edge of my area of authority, but I know it," he said. "What trouble are you talking about?"

"My landlord, Stanley Pickleton, has been arrested for murder."

His grumpy expression swiftly faded. "Who died?"

"Arthur Blackstone," I said. "I don't know many details, but Uncle Harry heard from an inside source about the murder and let me know because of my connection to the Dripping Tap. Apparently, Arthur's body was found outside the pub in the early hours of the morning. Stanley has been arrested. I spoke to Detective Chief Inspector Taylor about it."

He huffed out a breath. "If he catches you poking about in this investigation, it'll be a black mark against your name."

"I fear there's already one," I said. "I may have spoken in anger when our paths crossed. I went to the Dripping Tap to find out what was going on, and he was there. We had a small set-to. Nothing serious, but I got the impression my questions irritated him."

"I can't imagine such a thing possible," Inspector Templeton said.

I tutted. "All the man was interested in was Ruby. I could get no information about what happened to Arthur."

"Because he was doing his job."

"You always give me information when we investigate together," I said.

"So you don't keep nagging me, and I can get peace to focus," Inspector Templeton replied.

I quirked an eyebrow. "I never nag, simply sternly enquire and cajole. I ensure the right things happen at the appropriate times. There's nothing wrong with that."

Inspector Templeton slowly shook his head, exasperation clear in his gaze. "Arthur Blackstone was a local criminal."

"You knew him?"

"If it's the same chap, then yes. He was a former soldier, too. Dishonourably discharged from the army because he was caught stealing. There was a trial, and he was sent to Aldershot glasshouse. After he'd served his time, he returned to his roots in the East End. Ever since his return, he's caused trouble."

"It sounds like that trouble finally caught up with him outside of my pub," I said.

"It would appear so. I don't know your landlord," Inspector Templeton said. "Our paths have never crossed."

"Stanley's new. Been working at the pub for a year," I said. "I hired him when my last publican retired due to ill health. He's a hard worker, but I can't say we're friendly. It took Stanley ten minutes to get over the shock of being interviewed by a woman. Ever since, he's kept a wary distance from me. He does his work, and ensures the pub earns a tidy profit, but he's cut from an old kind of cloth and considers women in charge of any form of industry a strange affair."

"Would you know if he had a connection to Arthur?" Inspector Templeton asked.

"We never discussed his friends. Or his enemies. But Stanley provided a reference before I employed him. It was suitable."

"What about a criminal past? Did you check that?"

I pressed my lips together. "I was in rather a hurry to fill the position, and didn't want to leave the pub closed for long. I trusted my instincts. They're never wrong."

"I've seen them go astray a time or two."

"You must be thinking of someone else." I helped myself to a third chocolate, then placed the lid on the box to avoid temptation.

"As interesting as this is, I'm unsure how I can help," Inspector Templeton said. "I'm not on active duty, and I can't leave my hospital bed to go to the station and find out what's going on."

"I'm not asking for that," I said, "but I would appreciate you getting an officer to provide me with a list of Arthur's local contacts. I'll ask around and see if anyone had any issues with him."

"No, that's dangerous," Inspector Templeton said. "Arthur was unsavoury. He had deep connections in the East End criminal underworld that span decades. If you poke around there, you'll get in trouble, and I won't be able to extract you from it."

"I barely ever need extracting from trouble," I said. "And if it finds me, I'll deal with it. I don't want Stanley charged with a crime he didn't commit."

"Since you don't know him well, you can't be certain he didn't do it," Inspector Templeton said. "For all you know, he has a history of violence and an issue with Arthur. The two clashed outside the pub, and Stanley went too far. This is the result."

"At this early stage in the investigation, I'm unwilling to accept that," I said. "So should you."

Inspector Templeton heaved out a sigh, then winced and wrapped a hand around his ribs.

I leaned over him. "Are you in pain? Can I do anything to make you more comfortable?"

"No, there's nothing they can do for cracked ribs. I need to rest and let them heal. Shallow breaths help."

"Then the less sighing you do around me, the better," I said. "I'll keep myself safe, but I need access to information only you can provide."

"I don't like this," Inspector Templeton said after several seconds of contemplation. "While I respect your interest in supporting your employee, let the police do their job. They'll investigate the scene, interview Stanley, and if they don't have enough evidence, they'll release him. It's hardly a surprise they took him in, since Arthur's body was discovered outside the pub. I'm assuming Stanley lives there."

"He has a room upstairs. But just because he was in the vicinity of a murder doesn't mean he did it," I said. "I'm certain there are several little old ladies who live close to the pub. They can't be considered suspects, too."

"They may as well be. Until I know more about the case, it's impossible to narrow down who murdered Arthur," Inspector Templeton said.

I flashed up my eyebrows. "Does that mean you'll help?"

The door handle rattled, and I dashed around the side of the bed and ducked out of sight. I didn't want a nurse scolding me for breaking the rules.

"I can't stop." Sergeant Matthers entered the room and strode towards the bed. "I snuck out two new case files. All the information is here to get you going."

Inspector Templeton cleared his throat. "Thank you, Sergeant. I didn't expect you to return this evening."

"You said you were going stir-crazy stuck in this bed. And I felt bad about going home without giving you something to keep your brain occupied," Sergeant Matthers said. "There's a suspicious death on Westgate Street near the loading bays, and a body's been found outside a pub in the East End. Rough part of town, most likely a brawl that went wrong, but I thought you'd like the case."

Inspector Templeton grumbled something under his breath and glanced down at me. "Get up, Veronica."

I stood, and Sergeant Matthers yelped and leaped back. "Blimey! You just about near gave me a heart attack. What were you doing down there?"

"She was hiding so a nurse wouldn't throw her out." Inspector Templeton flipped open a file.

"Good evening, Sergeant Matthers," I said sweetly. "Did you say you had the case file on Arthur Blackstone?"

"How do you know about him?" His eyes widened, and he scrubbed at the back of his neck with a hand. "I'll get in trouble if I'm caught talking about an open case with a civilian."

"We won't say a word," I whispered. "And you're not to blame for my superior knowledge. My journalistic prowess brought word there was trouble at one of my pubs."

"Oh! Of course. I didn't know the Dripping Tap belonged to you." Sergeant Matthers visibly relaxed. "That makes it fine to talk about, doesn't it?"

"It absolutely does. I'm glad you brought the file to Inspector Templeton," I said. "It's important we have the best people on the case."

Sergeant Matthers's gaze flicked from me to Inspector Templeton. "Everything is in chaos at the station. Cases are being ignored or dropped, and people kept in cells for too long. It's not just because Inspector Templeton is stuck in here neither, but we're several men down after the explosion. And ... I don't like to speak badly about Detective Chief Inspector Taylor, but he's yet to take the reins on all the cases Inspector Templeton was covering."

"I'm unsurprised to hear that," I said. "My recent encounter with him left me less than impressed with his abilities or even his basic common sense."

"Things will sort themselves out," Inspector Templeton said, neatly arranging the files and settling them on his thigh.

I couldn't hide my smile of relief. It was the first time there were no lines of pain or frustration etched across his face. "I'm glad you're taking an interest in your work. It'll take your mind off of everything else."

"I don't know about that, but I need something to do whilst I'm stuck in here. The wretched doctor still won't settle on a date for my discharge," Inspector Templeton said.

"So long as you don't overtax yourself, I see no harm in you assisting me and Sergeant Matthers to solve this murder. What do you think, Sergeant?" I asked.

He gulped. "I really couldn't say."

"Then allow me to speak for you. How do we intend to clear Stanley's name and find Arthur's killer?"

Chapter 6

"It was an award-winning performance." Ruby pressed the back of her hand to her forehead and flopped onto my mother's large bed.

We were all crammed around it, following our visit to see Inspector Templeton. Even Matthew joined us, unfortunately still dressed in a pair of crumpled blue and white striped pyjamas, his hair looking like it hadn't been washed for at least a week. But the lure of paper-wrapped, piping hot fish and chips was too much for him to resist.

"I'm not sure you should keep bothering Inspector Templeton in his weakened condition." My mother blew on a hot chip. "He needs time to heal. And I keep thinking about those injuries he sustained. He may never be fully recovered."

"Nonsense. Being given a purpose is helping him," I said. "He perked up as soon as he realised there was an investigation underway. He enjoys a good murder almost as much as I do."

"There's nothing good about such a grisly business," my mother said. "And Ruby, you should know better than to help Veronica sneak around. You could have got yourselves in trouble."

"I'll always help," Ruby said cheerfully. "If the police have the wrong man for this murder, then justice must be done. Isn't that what you always say, Veronica?"

"Absolutely right," I said. "Although I didn't like to admit it to Inspector Templeton, I know little about Stanley, so I feel partly responsible for this situation. I should have thoroughly checked his background before employing him to run the pub. What if I hired a criminal, and this is the result?"

"You can't blame yourself for what happened," my mother said. "The best thing you can do is stay out of it."

"But the reputation of the Dripping Tap is at stake," I said. "And its reputation was hardly golden before this murder happened in the gutter outside."

My mother shook her head, her lips pursed. "I never understood why your father bought pubs in those kinds of areas. They're not respectable, and it's no place for a lady to visit. Matthew, I wish you'd help Veronica. You should deal with the seedier side of our business."

Matthew busied himself with his food, his attention on his recently adopted puppy, Felix. "I was never into the pub business. Veronica has a knack for it. And she's a whiz with the finances. I'd mess things up."

"You'd have a knack for it too if you educated yourself in our business affairs. Veronica wasn't born knowing how to balance books and deal with irksome employees. You could learn a thing or two from her."

I patted my mother's arm, a gentle warning to stop pushing Matthew. I hadn't seen him dressed since he heard about Inspector Templeton's injuries. Although he didn't ask me any questions, he always listened intently whenever I mentioned him.

"Father always told us pubs were the heart of a community," I said. "You create a vibrant and welcoming place for people to drink, and it buoys the grimiest of parishes. Although the location of the Dripping Tap does leave something to be desired. Perhaps Father hoped the area would be regenerated."

"I expect it's at the bottom of a long list of places that need a boost," Ruby said. "With the battering London took during the war, there are so many places that need funds to rebuild and give vim and vigour to damaged communities."

"The East End was never well looked after, even before the war," my mother said. "It's why it attracts dubious types like Stanley Pickleton and Arthur, what did you say his surname was?"

"The victim was called Arthur Blackstone. We know something about Arthur's character, thanks to Inspector Templeton," I said, "but not Stanley. He could be an upstanding citizen."

"He wouldn't have been arrested so swiftly if he didn't have trouble attached to his name," my mother said. "Stanley is a bad sort. Although the man he murdered sounds no better. Perhaps he's better off out of the way."

"That's no way to talk about a man you've never met," I said. "And Arthur could have turned over a new leaf and forgone his criminal past. People can change."

"Turned over leaves looking for trouble, more like." My mother finished the last of her fish.

"Did Arthur like to box?" Matthew asked softly.

"Not that I'm aware of," I said. "Why do you ask?"

"I know that name. There was an Arthur Blackstone on the amateur boxing circuit. It was during the war. We'd hold friendly boxing matches between different squadrons. I never took part. I only watched, but that's where I know him from."

"That would be a good place to start," Ruby said. "There are plenty of boxing establishments around London."

"What do you know about such an unladylike sport?" my mother asked. "Boxing rings are no place for respectable women to be seen. They let harlots and women with an attachment to drink and trouble lurk around places like that. I know you like a martini, Ruby, but it's the last place I'd expect to find you."

Ruby blushed. "I dated a chap who was into his sport. He snuck me into a boxing match once. It was only a friendly spar. Some of his well-to-do friends went a few rounds and then headed to their private club for drinks. It was ever so exciting. All that bare flesh and all those sweaty men grunting at each other."

My mother clapped her hands over her ears. "Enough with the scandalous talk! You're to go nowhere near a boxing ring. Neither of you."

I had no knowledge of local boxing establishments, so I'd need to do my research, but I could start by looking for places close to the Dripping Tap. If Arthur was a regular at the pub, he'd most likely have lived nearby, so it was safe to assume he went to a boxing ring near home, too.

"Matthew, I don't like the look in your sister's eyes." My mother's tone grew shrill. "Make sure she does nothing foolish."

"No one can control Veronica," Matthew said with a resigned shrug, tossing me a half smile. "And that's a good thing, since she gets everything sorted for us."

"While I'm around, you barely need to lift a finger," I murmured. Maybe I was foolish for being so protective of my family. If they were less mollycoddled, my mother and Matthew would be forced to venture into the great outdoors and tend to their own needs. But the thought of leaving them alone, potentially trapped in this house, was too much to bear. What if my mother's treacherous heart palpitations intensified? What if Matthew's night terrors grew worse? I couldn't have that on my conscience.

"It's unlikely we'll need to go near any boxing matches," Ruby said. "While Inspector Templeton is incapacitated, his helpful sergeant, Sergeant Matthers, has stepped up. He's been sneaking information into the hospital, so I'm sure he'll help us locate any boxing club Arthur was connected to."

"He may not have the time to help us," I said. "From all accounts, the station is in disarray since Inspector Templeton was injured along with several of his colleagues."

"He's a sweetie, so he'll make time for us," Ruby said. "And when he learns we're considering visiting boxing clubs alone, he'll make sure we're protected. After all, it's a part of his job."

"You must not bother him," my mother said. "I forbid you from sneaking in anywhere where there are half-naked sweaty men being brutal to each other."

"How about I borrow a camera and bring you some photographs?" Ruby teased.

Matthew grimaced while Ruby chortled at my mother's alarm.

"We'll take the utmost care." I screwed up my empty fish and chip wrapper and fed the last few scraps to Benji, who'd waited patiently by the side of the bed, attempting to teach our boisterous new pup how to behave when there was delicious food around. "But I'm glad to say this business has cheered Inspector Templeton up."

"And he'll be getting the best care. Hospitals do wonders these days," my mother said. "I just wish they'd find a cure for my ailments so I could get out of this wretched bed once and for all. But my heart still thunders and my ears ring constantly. And don't get me started on my tremors. So many tremors."

"Is your doctor not taking care of you?" Ruby asked.

"He does his best, but he can't understand the cause of my troubles," my mother replied. "I endure them the best I can, but it never gets easier. Matthew, if you're finished with those chips, pass them to me."

I leaned in close to Ruby as my family squabbled over the last of the food. "If my mother had more things to think about than her racing heart, she'd recover much more quickly. Perhaps we should set her to work looking for dubious boxing clubs."

Ruby gave me a knowing look. She was well acquainted with my mother's health foibles.

"As soon as Inspector Templeton is well enough, we must have him over for dinner again," my mother said. "And he needs to rearrange a date to take you out for the evening, Veronica. I remember the look on your face when you realised you wouldn't be dancing with him."

"My expression had nothing to do with the failed attempt at a formal business arrangement with the inspector," I murmured. Although I had been surprisingly miserable about missing the ball and not going with Inspector Templeton.

Ruby sighed. "I was so excited about the Policeman's Ball. I spent two weeks' wages on a new dress, but I haven't taken it out of the wardrobe since it all happened."

"You looked lovely that evening," my mother said, "even though your makeup was smeared because you cried so much."

I repressed a groan. "Let's not focus on dinners, or second dates, or inviting people over. All we need to do is focus on the Dripping Tap, make sure Stanley doesn't go down for a crime he didn't commit, and find out everything we can about Arthur Blackstone and who wanted him dead."

I was up bright and early the next morning, and got to the newspaper office an hour before my usual time to make up for the lost hours yesterday. I'd actually been able to concentrate, and had whizzed through a pile of obituaries, barely noticing it was lunchtime until my stomach and Benji alerted me to the fact we were late to eat.

I needed to use my break wisely, though. I was on a mission to find boxing clubs near the Dripping Tap. I'd made enquiries via the telephone directory, and then turned my attention to the sports section of the newspaper. We didn't carry a full directory of local gatherings, but I found several boxing clubs and telephoned the owners to see if they knew of any clubs in the East End near the pub.

I discovered several addresses, and had numerous places to visit to track down information about Arthur and get the full measure of his character, and learn about any enemies he may have acquired along the way.

"Are you thinking of taking up a new sport?" Uncle Harry appeared by my shoulder, reading through my scribblings.

There was no point in covering the information with a hand, so I let him look. "I've found a connection to Arthur. Matthew thinks he boxed when he was in the army. There was a soldier of the same name who took part in contests."

Uncle Harry grunted. "What does that have to do with you? We'd agreed you weren't getting involved."

"I recall we discussed Arthur's tragic death, but I don't remember making any agreement about what I would or wouldn't do next."

Uncle Harry gently massaged his forehead with the tips of his fingers. "Is there anything I can do to dissuade you from being involved in this investigation?"

"If you can convince the police to let Stanley go and assure me he's a free man, I'll look no further."

"That's not within my power. It wouldn't even be within Inspector Templeton's power if he was on his feet and in charge of this investigation."

"Then the answer is no." I set down my pencil. "I assure you, I'll be discreet. Arthur could have made enemies on the boxing circuit. Perhaps he went up against the wrong opponent. If we can find out who he recently fought, that will give the police new leads, and they'll stop looking so closely at Stanley."

"Have you even talked to Stanley to see if he wants your interference?"

"You call it interference, I call it help. And no, I visited the police station, but Stanley was being processed and interviewed, and he was allowed no visitors. I must try again, though. I need to get the full measure of the man and make sure he knows he's being looked after. My father would do no less for him."

Uncle Harry heaved out a sigh. "Never a truer word spoken. Let's get a move on then. I've got a busy afternoon."

"You're coming with me to the boxing clubs?" I looked up at Uncle Harry in surprise.

"Your dad would have my guts for garters if I let you wander into places like that unaccompanied. And before you say it, I know you can look after yourself, but some of the chaps in the boxing ring are a breed unto themselves. They love the fight, and they don't care who they're fighting."

"They'd never hit a woman."

"Don't be so sure about that. There are also some women who box in these clubs."

"Goodness! Female fighters. I've had to swing a fist a time or two in an emergency situation, but I'd never do it for pleasure or sport."

"Which is good. The less you're involved in that seedy world, the better. Give me a minute to grab my coat, and I'll meet you outside."

Buoyed by Uncle Harry's support, I was glad to make progress. I'd have gone to the clubs with just Benji, but boxing was a man's world, so they'd entertain the presence of a strange man much more than me and Benji.

An hour later, Uncle Harry stopped his Ford Model-T outside the third club we were investigating, Dukes Boxing Emporium. The sign was shabby, but the paintwork was fresh. One of the main doors was open, and several men strode in whilst we watched, their expressions purposeful as they went to pummel each other in the ring.

"Remember what I told you. Let me do the talking," Uncle Harry said. "The last chap we spoke to almost burst a blood vessel when you asked too many questions."

"Forgive me, but I'm impatient. I sometimes forget myself."

"Don't forget yourself in here. It goes against your nature to keep quiet and behave demurely, but it could save us trouble. Much like you, I've thrown a punch a time or two, but if I can avoid it, I will. There's no point in getting a broken nose or a cracked tooth. Neither is pleasant nor easy to heal."

"You have my word. I'll be as quiet as a church mouse."

"A chatty church mouse with an inability not to squeak when she shouldn't."

I smiled as we climbed out of his vehicle and walked inside. I remained a step behind Uncle Harry with Benji in a show of deference, pretending to appear timid.

Dukes Boxing Emporium was a large open space with one main boxing ring in the centre of the room. Around the edge were what looked like training zones, with punch bags and heavy weights. There were several men skipping, all bare-chested. They watched as I passed them, and none of the gazes were friendly.

Uncle Harry stopped and asked if any of them knew Arthur. They all shook their heads or grunted in the negative. We'd received the same response in the last two boxing clubs. Nobody wanted to talk.

We completed a circuit of the room in less than fifteen minutes and gathered nothing helpful. Perhaps we were on the wrong path, or the information Matthew had was out of date, and Arthur hadn't continued to box once he left the army.

"This is the last place within a ten-mile radius of the Dripping Tap." Uncle Harry guided me towards the door, Benji on my other side. "This delve into the world of boxing has brought us to a dead end."

I flared my nostrils, instantly regretting inhaling deeply as a heady aroma of body sweat and unwashed feet invaded my nose.

"It was a good effort, though," Uncle Harry said. "Let's take a step back, wait and see what the police pull up next."

"I hear you've been asking about Arthur." A man stood in an open doorway close to the exit, his hair freshly washed, his face glowing from a recent bout of exercise.

Uncle Harry nodded. "Do you know anything about him?"

"Maybe I do. Are you the police?" His gaze settled on me.

"Journalists," Uncle Harry said. "We've got questions about Arthur and thought he might be local to this club since he drank at the Dripping Tap."

"He's local, all right. I'll tell you about him if you buy me a pint."

"That's a fair deal," Uncle Harry said. "What do you know about him?"

"He enjoys bare-knuckle fighting." The man's gaze returned to me. "And I should warn you, that murky world ain't pretty."

Chapter 7

Our new acquaintance, who'd introduced himself simply as Jimmy, took us on a short walk to a pub called the Spread Eagle. It wasn't one of mine. If I owned such a place, the outside would be immaculate, and there wouldn't be a poor chap face down in a display of dead flowers outside the entrance.

Jimmy opened the door, and a waft of smoke and stale beer drifted out. "I'll have a pint of beer. And a whiskey. There are tables at the back where we can talk without anyone else getting involved."

Uncle Harry kept his hand on the small of my back as we walked to the bar. Normally, such a situation wouldn't perturb me, but all eyes were on us as we waited to be served, and those gazes were hostile. And I was the only woman in the place, so I knew better than to cause a scene.

We got our drinks and found Jimmy sitting by a small round table set against one window. The glass was so grimy, you could barely see outside. He accepted his drink with a nod and took a large sip from his beer.

"How long have you known Arthur?" I asked.

If Jimmy was surprised by me presenting a question, he didn't show it. "Ever since he was a wee lad. I've got ten years on him, but we grew up on the same street, so I'd often see him hanging about on the corner and getting up to mischief."

"And you're both involved in bare-knuckle fighting?" Uncle Harry asked.

Jimmy lifted a finger. "Everything I'm about to tell you is off the record. My name stays out of this."

"We may be journalists, but we're not looking for a story about the fights," I said. "There was an incident at a nearby pub, the Dripping Tap. Arthur was involved."

"I heard a rumour he got himself into trouble," Jimmy said.

"It was more than trouble," Uncle Harry said. "I'm sorry to tell you this, but Arthur is dead."

Jimmy exhaled noisily through his large nostrils and downed half his pint. He thumped the glass on the table. "It's no surprise this day has arrived, but I'm not happy about it. Trouble always found Arthur. Wherever he went, it lurked over his shoulder, looking to strike."

"He was bound to find trouble if he was involved in illegal fights," I said. "Bare knuckle, you said."

"You could be right about that. And he had a temper, but it served him well in the boxing ring. He was fast and mean. And he wasn't averse to playing dirty when there was a lot of money on the table."

"That's how Arthur earned his living?" Uncle Harry asked.

"There wasn't much else for him to do. He found himself in some bother with the police. And then there was the business in the army. Why would anyone hire a crooked squaddie who kept taking what didn't belong to him?" Jimmy shook his head. "There was only one thing he was good at, so he used his talents to keep his head above water."

"Did you ever fight him in the ring?" I asked.

"No, we're a different weight class. Arthur was lean, whereas I'm more of a heavyweight."

"Do you know if he recently had a disagreement with anyone?" Uncle Harry asked. "A fight that went wrong? Someone holding a grudge because he beat them in the ring?"

"Arthur had a lot of wins under his belt, so that put noses out of joint," Jimmy said. "It could be that someone came after him. You said it happened at a nearby pub?"

Uncle Harry nodded. "He was found outside the Dripping Tap late at night. We don't yet know the cause of death, but the police are treating it as suspicious."

"Fighters settle their problems in the ring," Jimmy said. "If I ever have an issue with someone, we sort our differences with our fists. It's unlikely anyone would have snuck up on Arthur in the dark. It's not how we handle our business."

"Have you ever come across a fighter called Stanley Pickleton?" I asked.

"I don't know that name." Jimmy's hands flexed into fists. "Did he attack Arthur?"

"I'm certain he didn't, but the police are interested in him," I said. "I wondered if he was involved in the illegal fights, too."

"Keep your voice down." Jimmy glanced over my head. "We don't like everyone knowing about the matches. If word gets back to the Old Bill, they'll shut us down. I earn a few bob helping out in the boxing club, but it's not enough to live on, so I need my winnings from the fights to stay afloat. Arthur was the same. He lived a basic life, rented a room in a lodging house not far from here, and he scraped by. None of us does this for a life of luxury. We do it because we have to. We need it."

"My apologies," I murmured. "I'd be interested in knowing when the next fight is taking place."

Jimmy snorted a laugh. "As if I'd tell you. Besides, it's no place for a lady. What's your connection to this business, anyway? If you're not writing a story, what do you get out of it?"

"We're concerned the police are looking at the wrong man," Uncle Harry said. "And our family is involved in the pub trade."

Jimmy's eyebrows rose. "You own the Dripping Tap?"

"Not personally," Uncle Harry said. "But it's in the family. You must understand a death outside the pub is bad for business. Like you, we need a steady income to keep our heads above water."

Jimmy's smile was cold. "You both look like you're doing fine." He tipped back his head and sighed. "I liked Arthur. He was a hothead, though. He was dragged up rough, but I hoped he'd get out and make something of himself. Then he got called up to serve. He came back bitter and cold. He never talked much about the war, but he was never the same after that. His temper was even worse."

"That must have been hard, seeing your friend struggle," I said.

"I tried to help, but Arthur was past saving," Jimmy said. "All I could do was keep an eye on him and make sure he didn't go after anyone too dangerous. Looks like I failed at that task, though."

Despite asking in several ways, Jimmy refused to provide details about the bare-knuckle fights, although he did give us an address for where Arthur had lodged. I could understand his hesitation in providing more information, but the more I learned about the seedy business of bare-knuckle fighting, the more I realised Arthur had most likely tangled with the wrong person at a fight, which was how he'd ended up in the gutter outside the Dripping Tap.

We finished our drinks, said goodbye to Jimmy, and left the smoky pub.

"That was a solid lead to follow up," Uncle Harry said as he walked with me back to the car with Benji. "We can pass the information to the police."

"I agree. This gives us the perfect reason to visit the police station," I said. "And while we're there, we'll insist on speaking to Stanley. I want to know if he was involved in these illegal fights."

Uncle Harry opened the passenger door for me. "I won't waste my breath trying to change your mind. Perhaps if you see Stanley for yourself, you can decide his innocence or guilt."

I settled into the seat, checked Benji was comfortable on the back seat, and waited for Uncle Harry to join me inside the car. "I wish I had your confidence, but I don't know Stanley. And I'd appreciate you staying with me. He's more of a man's man. I make him uncomfortable."

Uncle Harry chuckled as he pulled the car into the light traffic. "There are few people you don't intimidate.

You've got me for one more hour, but then I must get back to work."

"You need to take a break sometime."

"The news waits for no man or woman. Besides, what else have I got to do?" Uncle Harry's wife, my Aunt Sophie, had left him years ago, taking their two children with her. Since then, he'd poured his energy into the newspaper, often to the detriment of his health.

Still, I was hardly one to lecture on that predicament. If my mother didn't nag me so fiercely, I wouldn't be home until midnight most evenings.

The twenty-minute car ride ended with us arriving outside the police station. I asked to see Sergeant Matthers, and we waited several minutes before he appeared.

"Miss Vale! What can I do for you?" He strode into the reception waiting area.

"We were hoping to see Stanley," I said after I'd introduced him to my uncle. "The last time I came, he was still being interviewed, but I'd like to know how he's doing, and ask him a few questions."

Sergeant Matthers grimaced. "I'm not sure that's a good idea. I'm not in charge of this case."

"I'm aware Detective Chief Inspector Taylor is leading," I said. "I'm also very aware he's most likely taking a meeting on the golf course or at a private club."

A smile flashed across Sergeant Matthers's face. "He's gone for the day. He was talking about taking some young lady out. He wasn't all that polite about her, neither."

"I imagine not. I promise we'll be discreet. But we have new information that's relevant to the case. It could help you find out what happened to Arthur."

With that nugget of a promise, Sergeant Matthers relented. "Come through. Stanley is being kept here for now. Detective Chief Inspector Taylor wants to charge him for the murder, but we need more evidence, or a confession. That's what he's pressing for. He poked at Stanley for almost an hour, asking him again and again why he killed Arthur."

I followed Sergeant Matthers through the door with Uncle Harry and Benji. "What did Stanley tell him?"

"He kept saying the same thing. He didn't do it. He knew Arthur, and they weren't friendly, but he had no reason to want him dead."

I glanced at Uncle Harry. We may know the connection between them, but I wasn't blurting it out until I'd spoken to Stanley to see how much information he was willing to share.

Sergeant Matthers settled us in a small, slightly bleach-scented interview room and headed off to collect Stanley from his cell.

"May I suggest you lead on the questioning?" I said to Uncle Harry.

"Happy to, even though it'll cause you physical pain to watch me do it."

I arched an eyebrow. "It's for the best. I know the measure of this man, so I'm sure we'll get more out of him with you here. I may drop in the occasional question, though."

"I'd expect nothing less."

Sergeant Matthers returned with Stanley. He looked surprised to see me as he shuffled in. He was a tall, lean, broad-shouldered man with a slightly hunched back and close-cut pale hair.

Sergeant Matthers remained standing beside the door, his hands clasped in front of him.

After a moment of hesitation, Stanley took a seat across from us. "I know why you're here."

"I don't know if you remember me. I've been to the Dripping Tap for a drink a time or two," Uncle Harry said.

"Sure. You're the reporter. Another Vale. Family member?"

"Harry is my uncle," I said. "And my father, his brother, owned the Dripping Tap before me."

Stanley simply nodded, resigned expectation in his weary gaze.

"We'd like to know what happened on the night Arthur died," Uncle Harry said. "I'm sure you've told the police, but we'd appreciate hearing it from you directly."

Stanley shrugged. "I can't get myself into any more trouble by telling you. I didn't like Arthur. He had a mouth on him and he drank too much. He thought he knew how to handle his beer, but he went too far. That night, he was causing trouble with my regulars, so I threw him out."

"You barred him?" I asked.

"No, he could return when he sobered up, but I keep that place respectable. It's a rough part of town, but I do my best."

"I have no doubt about that," I said.

Uncle Harry glanced at me. "What happened after you threw Arthur out?"

"I didn't see him again," Stanley said. "It wasn't a busy evening, so I called last orders, then everyone went home. I shut the pub and left as well."

"Where did you go?" Uncle Harry asked.

"I sometimes visit my old ma. She's not been well. I walked to her house. We talked for a bit, and I fell asleep on the sofa. I woke, she cooked me breakfast, and I came back to the pub. That's when the trouble started."

"You told this to Detective Chief Inspector Taylor?" I asked. "He knew you weren't at the pub at the time of the murder?"

"Him! He won't listen to anything I have to say. He thinks I'm guilty."

"They must set you free once they've confirmed your alibi," I said.

Stanley shifted in his seat. "My ma's not been well. I don't want her bothered by their questions."

"She'll want to be bothered if it means her son remains out of prison."

He shrugged and wouldn't look at me.

Uncle Harry leaned forward in his seat. "Do you know anything about Arthur's involvement in bare-knuckle fighting?"

Sergeant Matthers stiffened, and he focused more intently on the conversation.

"Wouldn't surprise me if he was involved in something as daft as that," Stanley said. "Arthur was a hothead and had no sense."

"What about you? Would you ever be tempted to get involved in illegal fights?"

Stanley's eyes narrowed as he glared at Uncle Harry. "I'm sure you know about my past by now. I'm surprised

I even got the job at the pub, given what I used to do. But here's the thing. I don't do that anymore. I know I hurt some people, but I had no choice."

"After your arrest, I was made aware of your criminal history," I said.

"And now you want me gone." Stanley slumped in the seat, his shoulders bowed. "Even though I do a sterling job?"

"You do an excellent job," I said. "It's my fault I didn't thoroughly check your background before employing you. And you've done fine work while at the Dripping Tap. The pub needs you."

Stanley looked startled. "You're ... you're not firing me?"

"No! We're here to help prove your innocence and find Arthur's killer."

Stanley ran a hand down his face and blew out a breath. "You really want to help?"

"Of course. But we need your cooperation," I said. "I didn't know Arthur, so we're having trouble finding people who had an issue with him."

Stanley considered the dilemma. "I can help with that. If you're looking for the person who did this, you need to talk to Arthur's snooty brother, Ernie. He's a fraud, and they hated each other. If anyone wanted him dead, it would be him."

Chapter 8

It was a good job I was an early bird, because I was up at the crack of dawn to get everything done before visiting Inspector Templeton and updating him on our progress.

One downside of my morning's adventures was I'd have to leave Benji behind, since my visit to the library and the hospital meant he couldn't come with me.

I crouched by the front door with Benji just before heading out. "Ruby needs your services. You must be on your best guard dog behaviour when you're with her. She's venturing into dangerous territory. She'll be by to collect you shortly."

Benji woofed softly, acknowledging the need for quiet, since I was creeping around so as not to wake everyone before leaving.

After giving him a treat and a quick pat, I dashed out of the door and found a taxi. Soon, I was alighting outside one of my favourite buildings in the whole of London. It was a treasure trove of information, and I visited the central archive at least once a week to uncover information about the dearly departed and their fascinating lives.

But I wasn't here for work. I planned on researching Arthur's brother, Ernie. From the information Stanley provided, Ernie was loved by everybody. And from all accounts, he couldn't be any more different from Arthur.

I'd telephoned ahead and gently persuaded the library clerk to let me in before official opening hours. Fortunately, we had a good relationship and a shared love of violet candies, so it didn't take much arm-twisting. And of course, the promise of a box of chocolates upon my next visit guaranteed me the entry I desired.

Once inside, I headed to my favourite desk, located in a quiet corner with excellent natural lighting. I searched through newspapers local to the area and military journals dedicated to London war heroes. It took me less than half an hour to find something relevant to Ernie Blackstone.

"Oh, my. Ruby is in trouble if she ever meets you." Ernie was picture-perfect handsome, with a chiselled jawline, a smart officer's uniform, and a twinkle in his dark eyes.

I read through his heroic service record, from him joining up voluntarily, rising through the ranks to sergeant, and finally leading the charge during a battle that ended up with the capture of more than a hundred German soldiers.

I jotted down notes, including information about the area he lived in and the good work he did helping wounded soldiers who'd not been as fortunate as him. Ernie was still in the army and had recently been promoted.

With a whispered goodbye to the library clerk, I caught a taxi to the hospital. What a stroke of luck! When I entered the corridor, there was no nurse at the nurses' station, so I strode along, my head up as if I had every right to be there. I tapped on the door to Inspector Templeton's room and crept it open.

He was sitting up in bed, looking as if he was waiting for me.

"You look brighter." I eased the door shut behind me. "Not in so much pain?"

"I had a good night's sleep," Inspector Templeton said. "And I've been thinking about the investigation."

"It's good to keep busy," I said. "Just as I have this morning. Has Sergeant Matthers been by to fill you in on what's been occupying our time?"

"No, but I had a note to say he'd be here shortly. What have you been up to?"

"I've been investigating a war hero." I settled on the end of his bed. "Arthur's brother, Ernie Blackstone. According to my troubled landlord, Stanley, he thinks they had a difficult relationship."

"How difficult are we talking?"

"We need to speak to him to find out, but it's a motive for murder. Ernie is a respected local citizen, still going places as his recent promotion in the army proves. And yet..."

"There's a stain on the family name."

I nodded. "Arthur was involved in bare-knuckle fights. Apparently, he fought to earn money. And he was incredible at it."

"Arthur was the black sheep in the family, and Ernie has ambitions that would be ruined if his brother's liking for violence was uncovered."

"My thoughts exactly." I pulled out my notepad and flipped it open. "Ernie is too good to be true. Not only is he a war hero with medals to prove it, but he's an advocate for wounded soldiers. He gives generously to charity. And he's handsome, to boot. No mention of a wife or children. He's an absolute catch."

Inspector Templeton scowled at me.

I returned his scowl with a coy smile. "Not that I'm interested. I'm too busy for shenanigans of that sort. But I was illustrating that nobody is that perfect. We all have foibles."

"Even you?"

I gently patted his hand. "Alas, I do. And I know you have them, too. All this stubborn business over wanting to be released from the hospital as soon as possible. I won't stand for it."

His shoulders tensed, and the scowl deepened. "I've told you I don't want you bothering me about personal matters, but here you are."

"And here you are, sitting up in bed, looking as bright as a button. That wouldn't be the case if I'd abandoned you to recover with not so much as a spot of light thievery to occupy you." I rested my hand on top of his. "And I never will. We don't always see eye to eye, but I respect you. There are times when I even consider you a friend. This is a terrible business, and friends don't abandon each other in times of trouble."

He blinked at me several times and opened his mouth to say something, but no words came out.

I stared back, unsure where this sudden urge to share had come from.

There was a tap on the door, and Ruby and Sergeant Matthers appeared.

Ruby stared at us with wide eyes. "We can come back if we're interrupting. I told Sergeant Matthers we should announce ourselves, but he said I wasn't supposed to be visiting Inspector Templeton, so we had to sneak in."

"Sorry, sir," Sergeant Matthers said. "We'll get a cup of tea while you and Miss Vale talk."

I'd already withdrawn my hand from atop Inspector Templeton's, and stood beside the bed. "There's no need. I was simply updating Inspector Templeton on our wonderful war hero. Arthur's brother is a saint."

"There aren't many of them around." Ruby joined us by the bed, and Sergeant Matthers stood at the end. "How well you look, inspector. Or am I permitted to call you Jacob again?"

"Shouldn't you be off somewhere, riding horses?" Inspector Templeton asked her.

"I should. But luckily for you, I've wangled the morning off from Lady M. There's a man visiting to talk about her summer holiday plans. She gets them organised through him. She's considering a trip to Newmarket. It's a popular area for horse breeders."

"Perhaps a holiday away from the horses might be nice for her," I said.

"She'd be bored if she travelled anywhere hot that had nothing to do with fillies. Although there was a brief mention of the Arabian Peninsula. Their horses are divine. Exquisitely bred and fast. Although made for racing, and Lady M is getting out of that business. She's more interested in stud work. That's where the money is."

"I'd settle for a week by the sea," Inspector Templeton said. "All that travelling would be exhausting."

"I'll put in a word, see what she thinks about the English seaside. The trouble is, the only four-legged beasts on our beaches are donkeys, and Lady M loves her horses. Anyway, I'm here to talk murder, not mares." Ruby looked at me, her eyes twinkling with repressed glee. "We've arranged to snoop around bare-knuckle fighting venues."

Both men exclaimed their horror and talked loudly for several minutes until I shushed them.

"If you keep yelling, a nurse will look in and wonder what's the matter," I said. "Fear not. We've taken precautions. Ruby will have Benji with her. He'll protect her if trouble comes her way."

"You can't skulk around some of the most dangerous parts of the East End with only a dog to protect you," Inspector Templeton said. "And Ruby will stick out like a sore thumb."

"I've dressed plainly," Ruby said. Her outfit was on the demure side, but she still had a jaunty red scarf around her neck and a delightful shade of matching lipstick.

"If you'll pardon me for saying, ladies don't go to places like that unless they're looking for business." Sergeant Matthers's cheeks grew red as he insinuated the inappropriate form of employment Ruby may be mistaken for plying.

Ruby tittered. "I'll be in a taxi most of the time, and if I have to get out and look at a venue, Benji will be glued to my side. There's something to this illegal fighting business. Arthur was involved, so we just need to find out who he tangled with, and then Stanley will be a free man."

The men stared at each other in silent exasperation.

Inspector Templeton huffed out a breath. "Sergeant, since Ruby is insisting on doing this, go with her. Wear civilian clothes. If word gets out, the police are looking for fight venues, they'll be closed and moved on before you've had a chance to scratch the surface of this problem."

Ruby flashed Sergeant Matthers a perfect smile. "What a treat. I'm getting a handsome chaperone, even if he's not in uniform. We'll have so much fun together."

"This isn't about fun! This is about bringing a criminal to justice and making sure you come to no harm," Inspector Templeton snapped. "Neither of you should be involved."

"But we are involved. You should be thanking us, not scolding us," I said. "We'll ensure a job well done. And it'll be a feather in your cap when the right man is caught. It'll also make Detective Chief Inspector Taylor look foolish for keeping Stanley in a cell for so long."

"That's something he won't thank you for," Inspector Templeton said. "Nor me, if he finds out I'm involved in this muddle."

Sergeant Matthers cleared his throat. "I telephoned Ernie Blackstone last night after we learned about his strained relationship with Arthur. I'm meeting him at lunchtime."

"Did he know about his brother's death?" I asked.

"He didn't, but he wasn't shocked by the news."

"Was he saddened?"

Sergeant Matthers's forehead wrinkled. "Ernie sounded relieved. He barely asked for any details, but he was happy to meet."

"Intriguing," I said. "Where are we meeting him?"

After a busy morning at the newspaper, I was glad to take a break at lunchtime. I'd had no word from Ruby or Sergeant Matthers about their progress in locating any bare-knuckle fighting venues, but I'd already arranged with the sergeant to meet in Mayfair, at a private members club Ernie had extended us an invitation to.

I arrived five minutes early, and after waiting at the entrance and seeing no sign of Sergeant Matthers, I went inside and announced myself to the smartly dressed middle-aged woman sitting behind the desk.

She left and returned a moment later with Ernie Blackstone by her side. We shook hands and made our introductions.

"I'm still getting used to women being in the police force," Ernie said. He wore an immaculate three-piece grey suit, his dark hair neatly swept off his face, as was the current fashion. He was even more handsome in the flesh.

"I'm not a police officer, but I'll forgive the misunderstanding," I said. "Sergeant Matthers will be joining us shortly. I occasionally assist the police with their investigations. As a journalist for the London Times, I have useful connections that help solve complicated crimes."

His eyebrows shot up. "Extraordinary. They need you to figure out what happened to my brother?"

Before I could take offence, the main door to the club opened, and Sergeant Matthers dashed in. He was breathing heavily and adjusting the buttons on his tunic. "My apologies. Miss Smythe was very ... demanding."

I pressed my lips together to hide a smile. I had no doubt Ruby put Sergeant Matthers through his paces as they investigated the sordid parts of London. "You're here now. I've just made the introductions."

"Please, come through. There is a room at the back where we can talk without being disturbed." Ernie led us along a velvet wallpapered corridor, a lush carpet underfoot.

We entered a small library. We were the only people in there, although Ernie double-checked to ensure we were alone, before we settled into leather seats, the faint smell of expensive cigar smoke in the air.

"I'm very sorry for your loss," I said. "Were you close to Arthur?"

Ernie sat forward in his seat, his elbows resting on his knees and his hands clasped. "We were brothers by blood, but that was the extent of our relationship. Our paths took different directions. I knew he'd end up here, but I hoped he'd have a few more years."

"You were raised in the same family?" I asked.

"Exactly. We were given the same lack of opportunity. I chose to make something of myself, and Arthur didn't. He even attempted to fake an injury to avoid serving in the war." Ernie shook his head. "It was cowardly behaviour, and I told him so. I volunteered to join up, and it was the making of me."

"Life as a soldier affects people in different ways," I said. "My brother served, and he's never been quite himself since coming home."

"It's all to do with strength of character," Ernie said. "I had it, and Arthur didn't. He was weak and swayed by temptation. That was his downfall, nothing else."

"You don't appear saddened by your brother's death," I said.

"He was a stranger to me. Arthur left home when he was fifteen. Well, he was thrown out by our late father. He caught him stealing from his wallet. I was glad it happened. We didn't get on when we were children. He was too quick with his fists. I'm the older brother by two years, but he still went for me whenever he had an opportunity."

"Brothers can have difficult relationships."

"There was no relationship." Ernie sighed. "What frustrates me is he didn't have to be like that. By the time I was fifteen, I had a job and was paying rent, while Arthur skulked about with a group of ne'er-do-wells and stole from his own family."

"It's strange how different family members can turn out," Sergeant Matthers said.

Ernie pursed his lips. "We lost touch after he was thrown out, and I had no interest in keeping the connection going. I cultivated a new and better life. When the war began, I saw it as my chance to shine. I worked hard to ensure I became an officer and a gentleman." He glanced around the opulent room, a look of satisfaction on his face.

There was a motive here. If Ernie learned Arthur had embroiled himself in illegal fighting, he'd have been concerned about family disgrace. It would have dented the veneer of a refined gentleman that Ernie had so nicely cultivated. What lengths would he go to, to keep everything he'd worked so hard for?

"May I ask what your alibi was for the time of your brother's death?" Sergeant Matthers asked.

Ernie looked askance. "Whatever for?"

"We ask all family members. It's often someone the victim knows who had a hand in the death."

Ernie clapped his hands on his knees. "It wasn't me! I took lives when I served, but that was what I had to do. I had no reason to kill Arthur."

"Even so, it would be helpful," Sergeant Matthers said. "To eliminate you from our enquiries."

Ernie sighed again. "If you must. I was having dinner at the club. We have a small private venue next door. I'd have been seen in there."

"You were dining so late?" I asked.

"Yes! There's nothing wrong with that. I'm a busy man, so I take my relaxation time when I can. And I do some of my best work at night." He stood. "Now, if you'll excuse me, I have work to attend to. I'll show you out."

With the conversation brought crisply to an end, we had no choice but to follow Ernie back along the corridor and outside.

I stood on the steps with Sergeant Matthers as the door closed behind us. "Make sure you check that alibi. Just because Ernie claims to be an officer and a gentleman, that doesn't automatically make him innocent. He clearly despised Arthur. Perhaps they stumbled upon each other and a fight ensued."

"I'll make an appointment to visit the club's restaurant." Sergeant Matthers pulled a wrinkle on his tunic.

I grinned at him. "So, sergeant, what scandalous things did you get up to with Ruby?"

Chapter 9

To give Matthew the evening off from cooking, I stopped on my way home and picked up pie and mash from one of my father's favourite pie shops. It was a rare treat, since we tended towards plainer food. But I was hungry after chasing around half of London looking for suspects, and Ruby would be famished, having spent the morning with Sergeant Matthers and then rushing to work to deal with feisty horses and an even feistier employer.

I bundled through the door, calling out to Matthew about the food, which I left in the kitchen.

"Veronica! Is that you?" my mother shouted from her bed.

"Who else would it be? Sorry I'm late. Today has been hectic." I was grateful to kick off my shoes and hang up my coat.

"It feels like weeks since I last saw you. You're always sneaking out and not telling me where you're going." There was an anxious edge to my mother's voice that I recognised. She was on the verge of an attack of the vapours, as Ruby so succinctly put it.

I hurried into her bedroom to find her propped up on a pile of pillows, a half-eaten box of chocolates lying beside her and a mournful expression on her lined face.

"You know I sometimes keep odd work hours. The dead don't always conveniently expire between the hours of nine to five."

Her shaky hand grasped mine. "This lateness has nothing to do with your work. You're hunting for murderers again. Tell me everything, but don't make it gory. Well, a small amount of gore is expected. But I won't survive the night if I learn of all the dangerous things you've been getting up to."

I eased my hand out of her grip. "Ruby will be here shortly. She's bringing Benji back. I'll tell you everything then, so I don't have to repeat myself."

My mother lifted her chin and sniffed the air. "Is that Mr Crust's Pies I smell?"

"Nothing but the best for you. But only if you're feeling up to it, of course. Perhaps a warm broth would be more suitable for you."

"I'm always happy to indulge in a pie! Did you get the mashed potato as well? I don't know what the man does to that humble root vegetable, but it always tastes divine."

"Of course. Matthew is in charge of warming and serving."

There was a knock at the front door, and a few seconds later, Ruby bounded in with an equally enthusiastic Benji beside her. There was another round of greetings, while I snuggled with Benji for a moment, glad to have him back by my side. Then we squeezed around my mother's bed, plates on laps in a most undignified manner, and the delicious scent of piping hot meat pies filling the room.

My mother gestured for me to speak. "Don't keep me in suspense for a second longer."

"We've all been busy today, ensuring Stanley isn't charged with a crime he didn't commit. His protests of innocence seem genuine, but the police are still interested in him." I lifted the top off my pie to let the steam out.

"How did you get on with Arthur's brother?" Ruby asked.

"He has a motive," I said. "But he didn't hide his dislike for Arthur. They travelled different paths as they grew up. Ernie became a decorated soldier and has cultivated the air of a distinguished gentleman, while Arthur spent time dealing with criminals and getting himself in trouble."

"Life has a funny way of twisting and turning." My mother scooped a forkful of hot mashed potato. "Those two boys are examples of that. One becomes a hero and the other a menace."

"Sergeant Matthers is checking Ernie's alibi," I said. "He said he was dining at his private members club so it'll be easy to know if he's lying."

"Is there anybody else you're considering?" Matthew asked.

"There is," Ruby said. "I spent the morning with Sergeant Matthers, whose first name is Rodney, isn't that adorable? Rodney and Ruby sleuthing together. We were searching for illegal fight clubs. And ... we have a lead on a venue."

My mother's fork clattered onto her plate.

Ruby looked around with a conspiratorial glint in her eyes. "The word on the street is Finn Grey runs the bare-knuckle fights in the East End. He's the man we must speak to."

My mother flapped a hand in the air. "I forbid it. The only type of men you'll meet at an illegal fight venue are the sort who have no respect for ladies. You'll end up in terrible trouble."

"Edith, I took the utmost care," Ruby said. "Not only did I have the fearless Benji with me, but a very capable Rodney hovered so close, I had a second shadow. He's ever so sweet. And he's dating a local girl called Sally. I couldn't get all the information out of him about their relationship, but he seems serious about her. I wouldn't be surprised if those two don't wed soon."

I could easily imagine Ruby prying out Sergeant Matthers's private details. She had a tenacious interest in everyone's personal affairs.

"That's all well and good, but you can't expect the police to chaperone you all the time," my mother said. "And with Inspector Templeton still in the hospital, it's too risky to continue this investigation."

"We must find other suspects," I said. "The police remain fixated on Stanley, and that's wrong."

My mother furiously dug into her pie, stabbing it so savagely I wondered if it had done something to offend her. "I have a mind to put my foot down. No daughter of mine should lurk around fight venues. And Ruby, if I were to tell your parents about this, they would say the same thing."

"Leave Ruby's family out of this," I scolded. "As much as I adore you, and will respect your wishes as often as they're practical, I refuse to let an innocent man be charged with a crime he didn't commit. And before you say anything, yes, Stanley is problematic, but he runs a solid business. I believe him when he tells me he's innocent."

"You don't know the man!"

"You should have seen the relief on Stanley's face when he realised he had people on his side," I said. "Until then, everyone looked at him as if he was guilty. And Detective Chief Inspector Taylor has been badgering him to confess. It's wrong, and I'll do everything I can to prevent an injustice from occurring."

My mother grumbled to herself, a large mouthful of pie preventing her from making more protests, although she'd be thinking of plenty.

"We went to some fascinatingly disgusting places," Ruby said. "Parts of London I've never seen. I was shocked by the squalor. I thought that business was being dealt with now the war was over. This country is back on its feet and life is rosy again. But some of the poor people we saw..." She shook her head. "Sergeant Matthers, Rodney, was ever so good. He was quick to give money for information and even helped a young pregnant girl of no more than fifteen who appeared to be living on the streets."

"The end of the war didn't erase our troubles," I said. "Many of us are fortunate to be in privileged positions, but the same struggles have returned. They were always here, but our attention was directed to ensuring our country's safety."

"Many people have it better than I used to," my mother said. "In Victorian times, there was no place for an unmarried woman to romp around town unaccompanied, getting herself into bother that could easily be avoided if only she listened to her elders."

"I'm grateful we've moved on from such stultifying beliefs," I murmured.

My mother's beady gaze fixed on Matthew, whose attention was on the food, while occasionally feeding scraps of pie to his puppy, Felix. "You need to help your sister. She can't go to these venues on her own."

"I never said I'd be on my own," I said. "And since Ruby has done such a sterling job, perhaps I'll send her back."

Ruby laughed. "I could go in disguise. Although I'm not sure I'd pass as a man. Perhaps I could try a false beard. My features are too delicate, though, for facial hair. Maybe I could stuff a man's suit and wear it. Or I could wear a hat pulled down low."

"I'm not sure that would be effective," I said. "Although a trilby could work."

"Girls! You'll be the death of me," my mother exclaimed. "Matthew! Promise me you'll go with Veronica and Ruby."

Matthew had shuffled to the edge of the bed, his plate clutched in his hands. "I need to let the dog out." He dashed away, ignoring my mother's protests.

I gave her an admonishing look. "Be gentle with him. Inspector Templeton's accident has brought up his trauma. You don't want him having a relapse."

My mother huffed out a disgruntled breath. "I don't know what to do with that boy. He never used to be this sensitive."

"We know why he's like this," I said. "I just wish there was more we could do to help him get back on his feet and start living."

Ruby's bottom lip jutted out. "I could find one of my single friends to entice him out. Matthew is handsome."

"He's not been involved with anybody since Isabella so cruelly abandoned him," I said. "She did an incredible job of splintering his already fractured heart. Thanks to her, I have a feeling he's given up on relationships." It would take a special woman to accept Matthew and his foibles. I loved my brother, but his quirky ways even tried my patience.

"Perhaps that's what he needs," my mother said. "A push into the real world. Are we too soft on him? You need a reliable brother if you continue doing dangerously foolish things."

"Nothing I do is ever foolish. And when there is a hint of danger, I always have support," I said. "Benji. Ruby. Occasionally Inspector Templeton. Matthew doesn't need to be burdened with this. We must be kind to him and give him as much time as he needs to heal."

My mother grumbled her way through the rest of dinner, Matthew not returning, leaving me to chat with Ruby about the terrible sights she'd seen while exploring the East End looking for fight clubs.

"Sergeant Matthers knows Finn by reputation," Ruby said. "He said he'd pull his file, but understood he was a man with fingers in a lot of pies, and not of the delicious savoury kind. There are rumours of him being involved in black-market activities during the war, selling stolen contraband at marked-up prices to desperate people. But he's always enjoyed running boxing clubs. Apparently, it went on during the war. The men who stayed behind, or weren't fit for service, occupied themselves in dubious ways."

"Did you get a glimpse of Finn?" I asked.

"No, but Rodney, sorry, Sergeant Matthers, got a couple of chaps talking, and they told us about the fights and who was involved. They pointed us in the direction of a venue just off Wandsworth Street."

"All this talk of illegal activities is making my heart flutter." My mother pushed her empty plate away. "This calls for brandy. I need something to settle my nerves. And Mrs Beacon brought round a chocolate cake this afternoon. Serve that, too."

"Delicious," Ruby said. "I've been famished all day. Lady M made me work doubly hard because I took the morning off."

Since Matthew had conveniently vanished, most likely hiding in his room and waiting for our mother to go to sleep and stop pestering him, I served the chocolate cake and generous glasses of brandy. It took an hour, but my mother eventually dosed off, the brandy proving a remarkable sedative when mixed with her medication. I'm sure the doctor wouldn't approve.

Once she was comfortably tucked in bed, gently snoring, I gestured Ruby out of her bedroom and eased the door shut. "We need fresh air and exercise after all that stodge."

"Should we take Benji for a wander?" Ruby asked.

"Yes, and Felix. But I thought we'd visit somewhere new." I pressed my finger to my lips, and we put on coats and shoes hurriedly, slipping out of the front door with the dogs. Felix was already remarkably well-behaved, having learned his manners from Benji.

It was a cold, crisp evening, with a full moon overhead as we hurried away from the house.

"What are you planning?" Ruby followed me onto the street.

"We're grabbing a taxi. I learned Arthur's address from that man I spoke to from the boxing club. He's renting a room in a dubious part of town. I want to see if Arthur's former landlady can be coaxed into letting us examine his personal effects. It'll help us to get the measure of the man. Maybe even find out how deeply he was involved in these fighting clubs."

"I'm glad you didn't say anything about this to your mother. She was worrying me," Ruby said. "Her colour is too high and her breathing rapid."

"She's got a lot to panic about," I said as we headed along the quiet street, most families sensibly finishing dinner and not plodding along the pavements. "Inspector Templeton is in hospital, Matthew's having one of his funny turns, and we're investigating another murder."

"Poor Edith. We do test her nerves," Ruby said. "But she sees that you always come back in one piece. And sometimes, Matthew appears almost back to his old self."

"My mother always was a worrier, even when my father was alive." I looked around for any signs of a taxi as we turned onto a busy street. "They were the opposite of each other, but it worked. He was too relaxed, and she was too driven by her nerves. When they were together, she geed him up, and he calmed her."

"They had an idyllic marriage," Ruby said with a sigh. "That's what I aspire to. A kind, loving, clever man. And handsome, too."

I smiled. "My father caught the eye of a number of ladies. They were always unhappy to learn he was married and very happily so. There's a taxi!" I lifted a hand, and a few moments later, we were sailing along the road, heading towards Wandsworth Common.

The street we stopped on was a sad, faded area, crammed with small terraces, most of which appeared to be split into separate flats or lodgings. We climbed out of the taxi and headed to the building where Arthur had lived.

It took several minutes of knocking before a woman in a housecoat and slippers opened the door. She was in her late fifties, her hair in curlers, covered by a headscarf, with a cigarette in her mouth. "I don't take ladies. This is a men's-only lodging house."

I held out some coins. "Good evening. We were friends with Arthur Blackstone. We'd like a moment with his personal effects. To say our goodbyes."

A hard smile crossed the woman's face as she grabbed the money and pocketed it. "If you say so, ducky. He didn't leave much behind, and little of value, if that's what you're after. Up the stairs, second door on the right. The police have already been, so I don't know what it's like in there. You've got five minutes, then you're out. And watch your dogs don't mess anywhere."

I thanked her, and we hurried up the grimy staircase, covered in a worn stained carpet.

Ruby pressed a hand against her nose. "What is that ghastly smell?"

"I suspect it's the dubious plumbing," I whispered.

There was a heavy smell of sewage and smoke in the air, and an underlying scent of greasy food.

I got to the door that would take us into Arthur's room. It was already open. The police must not have properly secured the room after they'd looked around. I pushed it open and froze.

There was a man loading items into a sackcloth. His head jerked up and our eyes met. He reared back, turned, and jumped out of the window.

Chapter 10

I dashed to the window, closely followed by Ruby and the dogs. We all peered out.

"He survived!" Ruby exclaimed. "It looks like he's damaged his foot, though. It's a stroke of luck he didn't snap his neck."

The burglar was limping away, the sackcloth slung over his left shoulder while his right hand was clamped to his thigh. I turned from the window and scanned the shadowy room. It was chaotic. Belongings were scattered everywhere, and drawers pulled out, their contents tossed around the room.

"We need to stop him." I raced to the door. Ruby was behind me with the dogs. We bundled down the stairs, causing the landlady to yell her alarm. I grabbed the knob and turned it. It wouldn't budge.

"Stop that bleedin' racket!" The landlady charged along the hallway, moving remarkably faster than her advanced years suggested she should. She held a large, greasy frying pan in one hand. "I run a respectable place."

"Your lodgings have been broken into," I called out as I tugged on the front door. "We found a man stealing Arthur's belongings."

"No one gets into this place without my say so."

"Somebody did," I said. "We intend to apprehend him. Please, let us out."

She hesitated for a second before pulling out a large set of keys. "Bring him back here so I can teach him a lesson."

"We will. And call the police," Ruby said.

"I don't want the police here giving my place a bad reputation."

"The burglar could be involved with what happened to Arthur," Ruby said.

The stern-faced woman hesitated again, then turned and lumbered back into the house, jangling her keys.

I raced outside and along the alleyway beside the last row of terraces, Benji and Felix keeping up with me easily. Although Benji knew this was a serious mission, Felix seemed to be having a jolly good time, his tail wagging as he trotted along.

"Wait up," Ruby called out, her impractical shoes slowing her. "I'm already getting a stitch."

"We can't let him get away. This is our man! He must know what happened to Arthur, so he came to gather the spoils."

"From what I saw of that sad little room, there were little spoils to be had," Ruby said. "It stank of unwashed clothes and stale food. And I doubt Arthur was wealthy, even if he made a few coins from the fights."

"Even so, whoever this burglar is, he knew Arthur wouldn't be home. Perhaps the reason he knew that was because he killed him. Keep up."

Ruby wheezed behind me as we sped out of the alley and onto the street. Our target was at the end of the road, looking left and then right as if deciding which direction to go to escape us.

"Benji, fetch." I pointed at the man.

Benji shot off like a well-oiled otter, his paws barely touching the ground as he chased down the enemy. Felix took off after Benji, still thinking this was a game. I had no fears about the young pup. Matthew trained him daily, and Felix took all his cues from Benji.

The man turned, saw the dogs approaching at speed, and yelped. He dropped the cloth sack and limped away.

I slowed somewhat, partly to allow Ruby to catch up, but also because I knew the dogs would do a sterling job and give me an opportunity to collect my thoughts and catch my breath.

Ruby shook her head as she drew in several deep inhalations. "The foolish fellow doesn't know what's about to hit him."

"It'll teach him not to take things that don't belong to him," I said. "But this is excellent. Could we have found our killer?"

"It does seem suspicious," Ruby said. "And he must have snuck into Arthur's room, since the landlady knew nothing about him."

"I have a feeling she keeps a sharp eye on her business," I said. "She knows everyone's comings and goings. I wonder how he got inside."

We reached the end of the road and turned in the direction Arthur and the dogs had gone. Our timing couldn't have been better. Benji launched into the air and slammed into the man's back, sending him to the ground. Felix was a few paw steps behind. He grabbed the man's trouser leg and gave it a thorough shake.

"Should Felix be involved?" Ruby asked. "He's only a puppy."

"A puppy who loves chasing down bad guys as much as Benji does," I said. "Almost as much as we do. Let's see what our thief has to say for himself."

By the time we'd reached the mystery man, he was curled into a ball. Benji had a firm grip on his shirt collar, and Felix was enjoying himself, shredding a trouser leg with his teeth.

"Pull them off me! I've done nothing wrong." The man's voice trembled with panic.

"We discovered you ransacking someone else's room," I said. "We have every right to bring you down."

"You're not the police. And those belongings are mine." He cringed away when Benji growled.

"If it was yours, why flee from us?" Ruby asked. "We caught you bang to rights. You were stealing Arthur's belongings. Why do such a dreadful thing?"

"I don't know what you're talking about. Let me go," he pleaded. "You can have the things in the sack. Take what you want. Just call off your dogs."

"We don't want Arthur's belongings," I said. "You're coming back to the lodgings with us. You have questions to answer."

"You can't make me. Two girls won't beat me."

"We'll have a jolly good go," I said. "And our expertly trained dogs will ensure you behave. They bite when ordered, so be on your best behaviour."

The man quivered on the ground for several seconds while Benji and Felix used him as a chew toy. "I'll come back with you. I didn't mean to cause no trouble."

"Very well. The dogs will release you, but if you run, I won't be responsible for their actions. They have a high prey drive," I said.

"I already said I'd come back with you. Get them off me before I lose a limb!"

I called the dogs away, although Felix took some convincing, since he was having such fun.

The man staggered to his feet and inspected his ruined trousers. "What am I supposed to wear now?"

"You could steal a new pair of trousers from somebody's washing line," Ruby said. "I expect that's where you got those."

The man's whiskered face crumpled. He looked around thirty, dark-haired, and scruffy. His clothes were poorly fitting, his trousers an inch too short for him, and his shabby shirt was torn in several places.

"You go ahead of us. The dogs will follow, and we'll be right behind them," I said. "The landlady of Arthur's lodging house wants a word with you. As do we."

After more protesting from our thief and walking far slower than necessary, we arrived back at the lodging house. We collected the sackcloth on our way to see what had been stolen. There was clothing, a pair of shoes, and a battered watch.

The landlady was waiting for us on the front step of her lodgings, the frying pan still in her hand. When the man got close enough, she walloped him on the side of the head with it. "The nerve! Breaking into a respectable place like this."

He cringed away from her and rubbed his ear.

"While we wait for the police, turn out your pockets," I said. "We want to make sure you're not hiding anything else from us."

"The police! You said nothing about the police."

"What did you expect would happen?" I asked. "You were caught red-handed."

"Unless you want another wallop, you'll do as the nice lady told you to," the landlady said. "Who are you, anyway?"

After several seconds of shuffling, he pulled out a small amount of money, a battered harmonica, and a dirty handkerchief, all of which he dumped on the ground. "Patrick Reid."

"Do you know him?" I asked the landlady.

She peered at him. "I've seen him around. Lurking about and waiting for Arthur."

"Did you know Arthur?" I asked Patrick.

"I know no one. Keep to myself. It's the safest way to be. If no one knows you, they can't cause you trouble."

"He's lying," the landlady said. "And I never forget a face. Especially not one that's covered in trouble. How did you get into my lodging house?"

"I didn't! They're not telling you the truth. I've never been inside this fleapit."

Benji grabbed Patrick's trouser leg and shook it. Immediately, Felix grabbed the other one.

Patrick whimpered. "Stop! I'll tell you what I know, but it's not much."

I called the dogs to my side, and they sat patiently, waiting for another opportunity to strike.

"Start with how you got into the lodgings," Ruby said.

Patrick's shoulders slumped. "There's a metal drainpipe at the back. I shinned up it. And the lock on the window doesn't work, so it's easy to get in and out."

The landlady raised her frying pan again.

Patrick cringed away. "I had a right to be here. I live here."

She huffed an angry breath. "You do not! I know all my lodgers, and you're not one of them."

"I've not been renting a room from you. I'm staying with Arthur, lodging in his room. I've been paying half his rent so I can sleep on the floor."

The landlady swung her frying pan, and it grazed Patrick's nose as he dodged out of the way. "These are my rooms. My lodgers aren't allowed to share. I make that clear before we do a deal. One room, one person. I can't have a place overcrowded. It breeds disease, and the toilet blocks if it gets too much use."

"I had nowhere else to go, and Arthur took pity on me. It was supposed to be temporary, but I've been here almost a month. I was trying to find work and a place to live, but there's hardly anything out there. Nothing that pays, anyway. If it weren't for Arthur, I'd be on the streets."

"That doesn't make it right." The landlady sniffed. "I shall have to put a lock on that window to stop it from happening again."

"How did you and Arthur get to know each other?" I asked.

Patrick looked around. "From here and there."

"Not through work, since you're not employed," I said. "What about the boxing club?"

Patrick's eyes widened a fraction. "I don't know about that."

"This scrawny little thing doesn't box," the landlady said. "A gust of wind would knock him over."

He puffed out his chest. "I'm in the featherweight league. I'm nimble on my feet."

"Not nimble enough to escape two ladies and their dogs," the landlady said with a snort of laughter. "Wait until my friends at the bingo hall hear this. We'll have such a laugh."

Patrick scowled at her, his whiskered cheeks ruddy with humiliation.

"Did you know Arthur through the boxing club or … the underground fights?" I persisted.

"Maybe. But what does it matter?"

"It matters very much," I said.

"Underground fights? You mean, illegal? I should have known Arthur was rotten," the landlady said. "If he wasn't already dead, I'd do him in for this. Taking such liberties is wrong."

Patrick shook his head, his expression sullen. "I saw no harm in being here. After all, what's a dead man want with his things? He can't take them with him."

I jumped on his words. "How do you know Arthur is dead?"

Patrick stuttered out several half words. "I … I just heard somewhere."

"It's not common knowledge." A thrill of excitement ran through me. There'd been no report in the newspapers about Arthur's murder. It was possible

Patrick had seen the police question the landlady and drawn his own conclusions when Arthur didn't return home, but it was unlikely.

"Were you at the Dripping Tap the night Arthur was killed?" I asked.

"No! I'll put my hands up to taking his things, but I had nothing to do with his death. Don't pin this on me." Patrick backed away, only stopping when Benji and Felix stalked after him.

"Do you ever drink at the Dripping Tap?" I asked.

Patrick's nervous gaze flashed along the road. "Of course. It's where all the local fighters go."

"So you do know Arthur through boxing," I said.

"I ... I don't know. You're making me confused. I need to think."

"What you need to do is give back what's not yours," the landlady said. "I'm owed rent, and the dead don't pay up fast. I was planning to go through Arthur's room and selling off anything I could, so I'm not at a loss. It's only right."

"Arthur may have family who'll want his things," I murmured.

"No wife or children. I always check. I don't want complications turning up at my door in the middle of the night. He was alone in this world. And I'll take what belongs to me." She grabbed the sackcloth and tossed it into the hallway.

Patrick looked on mournfully as she also grabbed the scant items he'd taken out of his pockets, although she left the dirty handkerchief.

A smart black police car pulled up outside the house, and Sergeant Matthers and a colleague joined us.

"Your timing is perfect," I said. "We believe this man is involved with what happened to Arthur. He knew him. He was secretly lodging with him. They drank together at the Dripping Tap, and he's also a boxer."

Sergeant Matthers took off his helmet and scratched his head. "Patrick Reid! Why didn't I think of your name when this trouble showed up? What muddle have you got yourself into this time?"

Chapter 11

I was at the hospital the next morning, under the pretence of giving Inspector Templeton an update. In truth, I missed our prickly interactions. No one stood up to me quite like he did.

"It was a stroke of luck Sergeant Matthers knew Patrick. He took him in after asking barely any questions. He had the measure of the man." I neatly folded a napkin and placed it on Inspector Templeton's chest, which he immediately snatched away and screwed up in his fist.

The napkin was tossed aside. "Patrick was born with trouble running through his veins. He's got himself into all sorts of mischief over the years, but I'm surprised to find him in the middle of this trouble." He scooped up a spoonful of cold cereal and ate it.

"Don't they provide you with a cooked breakfast?" I gave the cereal a disdainful glance. "You need the extra energy to speed your recovery."

"My stomach is still unsettled from the medication. They're looking after me well. You must stop fussing."

"As your ... friend, I have every right to fuss. In fact, just the other day, we were discussing what would happen to you once you left the hospital."

An eyebrow raised. "You're intending to be my nursemaid, are you?"

"If I must. You're a bachelor, and you have no family."

"What makes you think I'm a bachelor?"

I jerked back, a little surprised. "You've never mentioned a special lady friend. I assumed..."

"I never talk about my relationships because it has nothing to do with my work," Inspector Templeton said.

The thought of him having a special someone sat like a lead weight on my chest. Of course, I had no claim over Inspector Templeton, nor did I intend to proclaim one. And I wanted him to be happy. "Then she should be here, ensuring you're properly fed and arranging for your home to be suitably adapted for when you leave."

"Adapted for what?" Inspector Templeton asked. "When I get out, I intend to do exactly what I'm doing now. Resting until I no longer need to."

"Somehow, I can't imagine you following the doctor's orders. You'll be bored stuck at home in bed. Even if you have your lady friend caring for you. What is her name?"

"I always follow orders when they're sensible," he said. "Focus on the case, and not me. I'm surprised Patrick's name has been associated with this murder."

I sipped from the cup of tea I'd snagged from a tea lady as I'd snuck in to see Inspector Templeton. "You said he had a troubled life. Surely, it's no surprise it led him here."

"Patrick is a simple fellow. Easily led and never thinks through his actions. But he's not malicious, just slow on the uptake. He gets in trouble because other people encourage him to break the law."

"Do you believe somebody told him to do away with Arthur, so that's what he did?"

"Patrick's record has no evidence of violence. He steals, deceives, and has been involved with black-market dealings, but he's never hurt anybody. To go from theft to murder is a leap. A complete change in behaviour. It's not logical."

"I'm all for logic. Perhaps Patrick didn't mean to kill Arthur," I said. "They fought and something went wrong."

"Arthur boxed. And from what Sergeant Matthers has been telling me, he was excellent at it."

"Patrick boxes too," I said. "He's a featherweight."

"Which is a different class to Arthur. They'd have never met in the ring. And if they did, it wouldn't have been a fair fight. Patrick would have come off worse."

"Patrick must be the killer," I said. "He knew Arthur was dead, and the police haven't made that public knowledge. Uncle Harry hasn't even got around to considering an article about the murder. How else could Patrick have known Arthur was dead unless he killed him?"

"That is a puzzle," Inspector Templeton said. "Perhaps he overheard some gossip."

"I tried to find out how he acquired that knowledge, but hit a brick wall. I asked if I could sit in on Patrick's interview when Sergeant Matthers took him in. Imagine my surprise when he said I couldn't."

Inspector Templeton finished his cereal, a smile on his face. "What did you expect would happen? I never let you sit in on interviews."

"Untrue. You often do."

"Occasionally, I allow you to be involved if a friend or family member is in trouble. But that is all. As much as you like to think you are, you're not indispensable to the police force."

I lifted my chin and glared at him. "May I suggest you review that belief? If it weren't for me, you'd have a number of unsolved murders on your hands. I can't imagine Detective Chief Inspector Taylor would be too pleased about that situation. He may even call your competence into question."

Inspector Templeton dropped his spoon into his dish. "It's not true that the cases would never be solved, but you're always determined to be one step ahead of me. You delight in beating me to the punch."

"I'd say I'm often leaps and bounds ahead of you and your officers. I've prevented several innocent men and women being charged with crimes they didn't commit."

Inspector Templeton gripped the bedsheet. "I'm thorough and dedicated to my work. I'm far from incompetent. You're able to operate outside the boundaries of the law. That's why you very occasionally get to the truth before I do. I have protocols to follow, forms to fill in, meetings to attend. You're burdened with none of that. It doesn't make you better than me. It just means you get lucky."

I sniffed. "It's more than luck. But I never meant to imply you're incompetent. I've said on numerous occasions you do a solid job when not following the wrong clues or focusing too hard on a particular suspect. Success comes from keeping an open mind. I highly recommend it."

He took a large gulp of tea. "And I highly recommend that until you've been through official police academy training, you don't keep telling me how to do my job."

I glared at him, resisting the urge to smooth the rumpled clump of hair at the back of his head that had bunched up while he slept. "I meant no offence. I like to be useful. My job keeps me occupied, and watching over the pubs gives me a degree of pleasure, but there is so much injustice in this world. I like to think I have a hand in ensuring we get our man."

Inspector Templeton let out a gentle sigh. "I understand your motives. Life hasn't always been kind to you or your family. You like to get to the bottom of all mysteries."

"I have plenty of kindness in my life. Far more than many ever experience." Inspector Templeton was referring to my father's death, but it was something I rarely talked about, and certainly not with him.

An air of uneasy silence sidled around us, neither of us certain how to break this deadlock.

Inspector Templeton finished his tea. "I had good news this morning. The doctor on the early rounds took another look at my leg. He said if it keeps improving, I won't need surgery."

"Hurrah! That's excellent news."

"I'm not out of the woods yet, and I'll need a long stint of physiotherapy. It's also unlikely I'll be able to run as fast as I used to, but I'll be mobile. Fit for duty."

"I knew I'd see you back behind your desk in no time," I said. "It hasn't been the same without you. Sergeant Matthers is a decent sort, and Ruby's taken a shine to him, but things will feel back to normal once you're out of the hospital and stopping me from having fun."

"You can have all the fun you like. It'll take time before the doctor will sign me off so I can return to work. But I'm eager to get back," Inspector Templeton said. "Detective Chief Inspector Taylor is coming by daily to check on progress. He's worried I'll resign or won't be fit for purpose."

"If he thinks that about you, he's even more of a fool than I already know him to be," I said. "And he must give you the appropriate amount of time to recover. I'll be having words with him if he becomes a problem."

"It's a treat I'm sure he'll look forward to." Inspector Templeton's smile was wry.

"We must celebrate your good news," I said. "Perhaps I should arrange for a fish and chip supper to be brought into the hospital. Do you think the nurses will allow it?"

There was a light tap on the door, and Sergeant Matthers appeared. "Good morning. How's the patient doing?"

"Perfectly able to speak for himself, thank you," Inspector Templeton said.

"I thought I'd drop by before the morning shift starts," Sergeant Matthers said. "Give you an update on the murder case."

"Has Patrick confessed to killing Arthur?" I asked.

Sergeant Matthers shook his head. "We've run into a problem. Patrick is innocent."

I exclaimed my dismay. "He must be the killer! How else would he have known about Arthur's unfortunate predicament? Patrick is a known criminal. He was found in the victim's lodgings, robbing him blind, and he ran when we caught him. That spells guilty."

"I must thank Benji and his new furry companion when I get out of here," Inspector Templeton said. "Sergeant Matthers told me about the dogs' heroic endeavours in bringing down Patrick."

"Benji is an excellent dog," I said. "And I believe he's missing you."

"They should allow animals into hospitals," Sergeant Matthers said. "They provide great comfort to the sick."

"I'm not sick, just injured. Although I look forward to seeing Benji," Inspector Templeton said to me. He turned his attention to Sergeant Matthers. "Why is Patrick innocent?"

"He was nowhere near the Dripping Tap at the time of the murder. We've narrowed the time of death down to between midnight and one a.m. That's when a fight was heard. Several neighbours reported yells and heard things being knocked over. It went quiet after that. The autopsy also confirms the time of death."

"Does Patrick have an alibi for that time?" I asked.

"He couldn't have a better alibi," Sergeant Matthers said. "He'd acquired, no doubt by illegal means, some tobacco and bottles of alcohol. He was going around the local pubs, selling them. He got thrown out of several by angry landlords, and ended up on a street corner three miles from the Dripping Tap, trying to offload the last of his stolen items."

"That's close to the scene of the crime," I said. "Patrick could still be involved."

"His two very reliable alibis say otherwise," Sergeant Matthers said. "Two officers on the night shift got word of what he was up to and stopped him. I spoke to them, and they confirmed it was Patrick selling the goods. They found him, took the items off him, and moved him on."

"To where?" I asked.

"Arthur's lodgings. It was on their rounds, so they made sure Patrick got home safely and found himself in no more trouble."

I tapped a finger against my thigh. "Drat! But we're still left with the puzzle of how Patrick knew Arthur was dead."

"This is where Patrick revealed he's not as simpleminded as everyone likes to believe he is," Sergeant Matthers said. "Patrick made out he was going into the lodgings, but of course, he didn't have a key and wasn't supposed to be there. Once the police left, he walked off."

"To kill Arthur," I said.

"No, it was too late by then. Arthur was already dead," Sergeant Matthers said. "Patrick had a stroke of good or bad luck, depending on what side of the fence you sit on. He went for a walk, since he couldn't get inside without Arthur there to prop open the window. He said he threw a few stones at the window, but got no response to his signal. Patrick hung around for a bit, hoping Arthur would return, but when he didn't show, he went for a walk to keep warm. His walk took him past the Dripping Tap, where he almost fell over Arthur's body."

"Arthur was already dead when Patrick found him?" Inspector Templeton asked.

"Dead as a dodo. Patrick said he had a fright when he realised what he'd fallen over and who it was. But then he had an idea. Not a brilliant idea, but one that made sense to him," Sergeant Matthers said.

I sighed. "He took Arthur's personal effects, didn't he? And the key to the lodgings so he could break in without making a mess and getting caught."

"That's right. He wasn't going to look a gift horse in the mouth. He said a prayer over Arthur's body and emptied his pockets. He said someone was looking down on him that night since he had nowhere to stay. And because Arthur no longer needed his things, he made the most of the situation. Patrick spent the money Arthur had on a room at a small hotel, which I've already confirmed. Then he snuck back to the lodgings to load up with Arthur's things."

"Which is when we found him," I said. "Patrick had a sackcloth full of clothes."

"All belonging to Arthur," Sergeant Matthers said. "Patrick is a bad sort, but he's not our killer. He couldn't have done it."

"Double drat," I murmured.

How frustrating. There I was, thinking we'd got our man and had multiple things to celebrate, but this mystery was far from being solved.

Chapter 12

"What rotten luck." Ruby inspected the contents of her cheese and tomato sandwich that had been brought to our table in a small cafe where we were taking lunch. She set the slice of bread back on top of the cheese with a satisfied nod and took a bite. "Patrick seemed like the ideal suspect."

"I thought we were onto something." I looked at my own sandwich, cheese and pickle. It didn't inspire me. "But with the police as his alibi, Patrick can't have murdered Arthur."

A sensibly dressed elderly woman sitting at the table next to us stared at us in alarm.

I leaned closer to Ruby. "Stanley is still in the frame for murder. All our hard work has been for nothing."

"Not necessarily. We have fewer suspects to consider, and we still have the bare-knuckle fights that could lead us to more suspects. I'd say that's significant."

"True enough." I looked out of the cafe window at the bustling crowd zooming past on their break from work.

"Chin up, old thing," Ruby said. "You look like you have the weight of the world on your shoulders. I know you love to solve these mysteries quickly, but we're getting there. It's only been a few days."

"We always come through in the end, but this business with Inspector Templeton has got me thinking."

Ruby set down her sandwich. "His leg injury has you worried? Has he had a setback?"

"No, he's doing well. Although I had a stern word with a nurse about him being given only cereal for breakfast. They promised he'd get poached eggs on toast tomorrow."

"I'm sure she was thankful for your expert guidance."

I half smiled at Ruby's tart comment. "The nurse said she didn't recall me being on the approved visitor list, which was when I remembered an important appointment, and hurried out of the hospital."

"Inspector Templeton will be thrilled you're taking such excellent care of him."

"I find that most doubtful. I always thought no harm would ever come to us. Or him. We're not foolish women, and Inspector Templeton is usually careful when he goes about his business." I looked at my food. "I don't know what I'm trying to say."

Ruby caught hold of my hand. "I know what you want to say, but you don't have the gumption for it. You're fond of Jacob. And before you protest, I know it to be true. You're like children in the school playground. Neither of you wants to say how you feel, so you're pulling each other's pigtails."

"Somehow, I can't imagine Inspector Templeton with pigtails."

Ruby pinched the back of my hand. "You don't want to spoil what you have with him. You are friends, and that's marvellous, but don't you want to see what else you could be?"

"Mortal enemies?" I picked up my sandwich, then put it down. "I have been unsettled by his injury. I'm uncertain if he even likes me, though."

"He likes you very much. Why else would he put up with your sharp words and no-nonsense attitude?"

"For the same reason you do," I said. "It makes perfect sense to behave like this."

"To you, it does. And I think you're top of the pile, as does Inspector Templeton. But if one of you doesn't lower the wall a fraction, this will go nowhere."

"I don't want things to change," I said. "I like him, and I want him to be happy. Anyway, all of this talk is a waste of time. He as good as admitted he has a lady friend."

Ruby gave a less than dainty snort, earning her another glare from our nearby luncheon eavesdropper. "Unless she's an invisible lady friend, she doesn't exist. He most likely said that to gauge your reaction. He's as cautious as you about taking a step in a different direction. How did you respond when he told you about this make-believe relationship?"

"I said she should be at the hospital taking care of him."

"Much like you were. Because you genuinely care and you want to ensure Jacob fully recovers. His injury is a setback in his career, but it could be a step forward for the two of you. Now is the perfect opportunity to show him a different side."

"What side shall I show Inspector Templeton that he hasn't already seen?" I asked.

"Your softer side. You're full of kindness, but you reserve it for a select few people and any stray dog that happens your way."

I looked out of the cafe window, where Benji sat patiently, waiting for us. "Dogs are so much easier to understand. There's no subterfuge. If Inspector Templeton likes me, why can't he simply say?"

"For the same reason you won't say," Ruby replied. "You're afraid of being rebuffed. And Inspector Templeton is a proud man. If he made things official with you and you turned him down, his ego would be flattened."

"And therein lies the problem," I said. "If one of us makes a move away from friendship and that move is rejected, this is over. We wouldn't be able to see each other. I couldn't call on his services to gain access to information about cases we wished to investigate. Why make things complicated?"

"Because you could be blissfully happy together. I know you're content with everything you have, but adding a special someone to your contentment would make things even better." Ruby glanced at the door and frowned. "He's late. He's always late."

"Who are we talking about?" I was surprised by the sudden change in the topic.

"When you telephoned earlier and told me Patrick was innocent, I got to work on my own network."

"I didn't know you had a network. Were the horses useful?"

She swatted my arm. "I have connections other than my fine hooved friends, although they're usually only handy for knowing when the next party is occurring.

But I remembered somebody I used to date. Do you remember Harold Bennett?"

"That cad! I'll never forget him. He got so drunk at one party that he fell into an ornate fountain. Broke the head off a stone swan as he tried to get out, then made a mess of the lawn when he fell again and rolled around."

Ruby tittered. "He also tripped over a stone peacock and broke his toe. The foolish man was three sheets to the wind. Harold could never handle his champagne."

"And he stood you up twice," I said.

"He fooled me once, but when he did it again, I learned my lesson and abandoned all hope of romance and respectability," Ruby said. "But I've been trying to get information out of Sergeant Matthers about illegal fights and talking to the man in charge."

"I doubt he was helpful."

"Rodney was less than forthcoming."

"He's worried about sharing information for fear of losing his job," I said.

"Which is why we need Inspector Templeton back on the force," Ruby said. "Being that he's so hopelessly in love with you, he'd give you all the information we needed to solve this case."

"Let's not stray into the realm of the ridiculous," I said.

"I can assure you, as soon as he's back on the job, you'll be twisting him around your little finger to get everything you desire."

"Enough of that nonsense," I said. "What does your quest to learn more about the fights have to do with Harold? Don't tell me you've invited him here?"

"Exactly that! When I hit a brick wall with Sergeant Matthers, who point-blank refused to take me to an illegal bare-knuckle fight, I re-established my connection with Harold. He was supposed to be here ten minutes ago, though. I'd forgotten how terrible his timekeeping was. It's the height of rudeness to keep a lady waiting."

I couldn't hide my smile. "There's nothing worse than a person making you wait when you've scheduled an appointment."

And wait, we did. Fifteen minutes later, we'd finished our round of sandwiches and were on a fresh pot of tea when Ruby leapt out of her seat. "Harold! Over here."

I twisted in my chair as a handsome man with curly dark hair dressed in a pale suit approached. He was around Ruby's age and had a handlebar moustache and a slightly weak chin.

"Bunny! It's been too long. I was delighted when I got your telephone call." Harold's voice was upper-class crisp as he exchanged kisses with Ruby. "And Ronnie! Another treat. I didn't know you'd be joining us for lunch."

I carefully avoided his kisses. "It's Veronica. Nobody calls me Ronnie anymore."

"It suits you. You always have a strident, authoritarian air about you. Manly. Of course, there's nothing manly about your appearance." Harold chuckled as if he'd said something highly amusing as he took a seat, and Ruby poured him a cup of tea.

"I'm glad you could meet with us so quickly," she said.

"In truth, I was intrigued by our conversation." Harold snapped his fingers in the air. "Waiter! Desserts are required. Bring us anything covered in chocolate. My Bunny has a sweet tooth."

Ruby smiled, her lips pressed together as she caught my eye. "It's been some time since I've heard that nickname."

"It's your nose. Cute as a button. And it wriggles when you're annoyed. Which I seem to recall you frequently were with me, although I could never figure out why."

I inhaled, about to remind him of all the wrong he'd done Ruby, but she stepped on my foot and discreetly shook her head.

"You girls are interested in boxing, I hear," Harold said. "I suppose you're hoping to catch yourself a strapping champion."

"I do like a capable man," Ruby said. "As I'm sure you're well aware."

Harold puffed out his chest. "You couldn't get enough of my boxing stories when we were stepping out. I think I told you about my fight with Brigadier Baxter three times. Knocked him out so hard, he saw stars for a week and lost a tooth."

"Five, actually," Ruby said sweetly. "And that's why I remembered you were the man we needed to talk to."

"I was a champion at my university," Harold said to me. "Won all the trophies. And all the hearts. The boxing also came in handy when I did my bit during the war."

"Did you fight so close to the enemy that you needed to use your bare hands?" I asked in mock alarm.

"Hah! No, it never came to that. I was an officer, so I didn't spend too much time in the dirt, but it gave me confidence to know I could deal with any trouble that came my way. And the men were inspired by my stories."

"Of course they were," I murmured. I could imagine Harold living the high life while ordering the soldiers around, never understanding the full implications of war. I'd experienced my fair share of incompetent officers while serving. It nearly cost me my life on more than one occasion.

The waiter delivered three plates of chocolate cake, and Harold enthusiastically dug in.

Ruby took a genteel bite and set down her fork. "You were always so brave. And smart to use your skills to your advantage."

He preened under her praise. "I was happy to be of service. But tell me, why are you so interested in fights that aren't, how should I delicately put this, legitimate?"

Ruby fluttered her eyelashes. "Since the war, life has become dreadfully dull. I have barely any parties to keep me entertained. My work keeps me busy, but I need a thrill."

Harold chortled. "Naughty girl. You always were wild. It's one of the things I liked about you."

I swallowed my revulsion and followed Ruby's lead. "We both served, and we miss the exciting times that come with war."

"I'm surprised. You were always the sensible one, Ronnie, making sure Ruby didn't drink too much at the dances. And I remember you scolding me once."

"I suspect I scolded you on many occasions," I said.

Harold roared a laugh. "You jolly well did. And I jolly well liked it. Some men enjoy being taken in hand by a stern woman."

I made a fair attempt at eyelash fluttering, although it wasn't as effective as Ruby's expert delivery. "What can you tell us about these fights you attend?"

He finished his cake and leaned back in his seat, settling his hands over his stomach, a satisfied look on his face. "I work in the city, for my father's company. Finance. It pays well, but it's dreary work. That means I need something to look forward to. A place where I can let my hair down without ruining my reputation."

"A place where no one else knows you?" Ruby asked.

"Exactly. We have to keep up a certain appearance. My father would disown me if he realised I was sneaking off and watching bare-knuckle fighting in my spare time. But there's no harm in it. I like to place a little bet now and again on the fights, just for fun. And the people who attend are earthier types. They don't care who you are, just so long as you have money to spend."

"It sounds terribly exciting," Ruby said. "When is the next fight?"

Harold blinked several times. "Gosh! Are you serious? You really want to come to a fight?"

"I've been talking about nothing else to Veronica," Ruby said. "We need excitement, too. Times are changing. It's only right ladies attend such events."

Harold rubbed his chin. "I'll be frank with you, it's a rough crowd, and the only ladies you see there are those who sell a particular service."

"We'd never be mistaken for that kind of lady," Ruby said. "And if we go with you, you'll look after us, won't you? Harold will be our hero."

"Of course. It would be a privilege to take you both," he said. "Hmmm..."

"What is it?" Ruby asked. "We'll be discreet. We won't say a word about what we're planning or tell anyone where the fight is taking place. We're excellent at keeping secrets."

"It's not that. I trust you not to gossip about our little adventure. But I need to know, if I help you in this matter, what will I get in return?" Harold winked at Ruby.

"Two gorgeous, single women on your arm," she stated boldly.

He glanced at me. "Will we go dancing afterwards? I'm a member of a discreet private club. No riff raff. Plenty of champagne."

"Of course," Ruby said without hesitation. "Fighting and then dancing. The perfect combination."

Harold smirked. "I hope you ladies aren't easily shocked."

"Barely anything shocks me these days," Ruby said.

I nodded. "I've reported on plenty of stories that would make anyone with a lesser constitution faint."

"That's right. You're a journalist, aren't you?" Harold said. "You'd better not write about this."

"Veronica is only interested in having a fun time, too," Ruby said. "Isn't that right, Ronnie?"

I nodded and forced a smile.

Harold smirked, sensing my discomfort. "Then it's a date. I'll pick you both up at ten o'clock tonight. Make sure you dress to impress."

Chapter 13

"Going out so late on a weeknight is unbecoming." My mother trailed after me in her long white nightgown, her hair partially hidden under a nightcap, glasses perched on the end of her nose.

"It was the only night everybody was available." I dashed about, setting things in order.

"But you haven't told me where you're going or who you're going with." She followed me into my bedroom, where Ruby was still getting ready. My mother must be concerned, since she so rarely got out of bed.

"There's nothing to worry about," Ruby said. "We had a last-minute invitation to an exclusive venue with two eligible single men. It was an offer we couldn't refuse."

"You have gentleman callers about to arrive here?" My mother's gaze flashed towards the hallway. "You didn't say they were coming here. I'm not dressed!"

"Then it's fortunate they're not taking you out." I narrowed my eyes at Ruby. There'd been no mention of me having a date to take me to the fight. What had she planned behind my back?

"I've known my date a long time," Ruby said. "He's a little roguish, but charming. And he has bundles of money. He works in finance in the city. For a very respectable company."

"Oh! This is exciting." My mother's concerns vanished as she learned about Harold. "What about Veronica's gentleman?"

I remained silent, my steely gaze on my soon to be no longer best friend. I was also interested in this information.

Ruby lightly applied blush to her cheeks. "His name is Richard Talbot. He works with Harold. Different departments, I believe. I imagine he's just as wealthy, though. They've promised to show us a good time."

"Make sure it's a respectable good time," my mother said. "And I can't understand why they won't take you out at a more suitable hour. Surely, for a first date, dinner would be a better option."

"It's a sort of dance." Ruby flicked a guilty look my way. "I don't know much else about it. There may be food."

"It seems strange to me, a dance taking place at this time of night. Where is it?" my mother asked.

"The gentlemen arranged it as a surprise," Ruby said. "Aren't you happy Veronica is finally getting out and meeting respectable men?"

It was hard for me to hold in a disparaging snort. Harold and whoever he'd dragged into this evening's adventures were anything but respectable.

"Of course! But I've always had hope that Inspector Templeton would become a member of our family," my mother said.

"Mother! That's enough. You're getting yourself worked up for no reason." I firmly but gently guided her back to her bedroom. "We need to finish getting ready, and you need to stop fretting. It's a simple evening with two gentlemen. If it's no fun, I'll be home by midnight. Maybe earlier."

"I just want to see you happy." She caught hold of my hand. "You can be ever so serious, and with everything that's going on with Inspector Templeton, I've been worrying about you."

"I know. More than usual, but there's no need." I gave her a gentle hug. "Since you're up, sit with Matthew and have a nice cup of tea together. I've barely seen him since I got home from work. He only said two words to me when I left Benji with him so he could help to train Felix."

"No, I'm exhausted. And my feet are like blocks of ice. It's a sign I'm coming down with something unpleasant. Another bout of pneumonia, no doubt. Or maybe a variant on the black death. I was reading about that the other day. It's making a comeback."

"It is not! You should be wearing slippers. It's no wonder your feet are so chilled. Back into bed with you." I helped my mother get under the covers. Ever since Ruby and I had arrived home to get ready for the evening's investigation, my mother had been flapping around us like a wounded goose. But I was determined she wouldn't learn about our true destination, because her heart would palpate for weeks with worry.

Once my mother was settled, I marched back into my bedroom and settled my hands on my hips. "I didn't know I also had a date this evening."

"Don't be angry, but Harold contacted me as I was about to leave Lady M's. He said he had a single chap he wanted to bring along. He's been to the you-know-what before, so he knows what to expect. And I thought it would be sensible to have another man with us. If the fights are as rough as I suspect they'll be, we may need extra muscle."

"We're perfectly capable of dealing with any disreputable types that bother us," I said. "A kick to the crown jewels sends the mightiest of men to their knees."

"Harold was persuasive, and I didn't want him to change his mind about taking us. This could be our only opportunity to ask about Arthur and speak to the man in charge of the fights." Ruby gestured me over. "Hurry and finish your makeup. They'll be here in a few minutes."

"I'm ready."

Ruby tutted. "At least put on lipstick."

I gritted my teeth as she applied a discrete shade of pink to my lips.

There was a loud knock at the front door, making me wince. The noise would no doubt cause my mother's pulse to spasm. While Ruby went to let the gentleman in, I headed to Matthew's bedroom and lightly tapped on his door. I pushed it open to find him sprawled on the bed, Felix snoring beside him, and Benji sitting on the floor. "I'm heading out. Look after Benji for me."

Matthew nodded. "It's a funny time to be going out for a dance."

"Don't start. I've had Mother bending my ear all evening. We won't be long." I glanced around his bedroom, which was an eclectic collection of books, curiosities from his former hobby as a fossil hunter, and clothes that needed tidying. This was how Matthew lived. Messy chaos in head and reality.

After saying goodbye to Benji and promising him a long walk tomorrow as a reward for being such a good boy, I hurried out to meet my date. Ruby was chatting with Harold, and beside him stood a tall slim chap, smartly dressed, with an almost identical handlebar moustache.

"Here she is," Ruby said as she turned to me. "Richard, I'd like you to meet Veronica Vale."

He bent at the waist, grabbed my hand, and kissed the back of it. "A pleasure to meet you."

I noted his glassy eyes and slurred speech as I removed my hand from his clammy grasp.

"We've got a taxi waiting," Harold said. "We'd better hurry. We don't want to miss the first fight."

I collected my small, beaded handbag, which Ruby had insisted would be more suitable than the usual oversized affair I took into work, put on my coat, and we left the house.

Once we were settled in the taxi and on our way, I quickly discovered the reason my date was already slurring. Harold and Richard had large hip flasks, which they opened and drank from. We were offered a drink, but politely declined, the smell of strong whiskey turning my stomach.

"I'm surprised you girls want to come to the fights." Richard rested his arm along the back of the taxi seat, so it draped close to my shoulder.

"They're looking for adventure," Harold said.

Richard harrumphed a laugh. "They'll get it here. There are six fights tonight. It'll be a thrilling evening."

"We may not stay for all of them," I said. "We have work tomorrow."

"So do we. But a hair of the dog will see you right. Are you sure I can't tempt you?" Richard wobbled the hip flask in my face.

"Quite sure, thank you," I said. "Where are we going?"

"Sit back and let the driver do the work," Harold said, his eager attention on Ruby. "We'll be there in half an hour."

The journey took us away from the respectable parts of London and back to the downtrodden East End, with its worn streets and lopsided tenements. I tried to concentrate on where we were going, but Richard's chatter and alcohol-laden breath were a distraction. I could do without his attention, since irritating nerves rioted around my stomach like a kitten after yarn.

The taxi slowed, inching along an uncared-for road. "This is as far as I can take you. Any farther, and I'll blow a tyre. Some of these holes are lethal."

"Good chap." Harold paid the driver.

I was about to get out when Richard attempted to plant a sloppy kiss on my cheek. I jerked away and shoved him in the chest.

"Enough of that! Harold said you'd be fun." Richard rubbed his chest and smoothed his shirt. "I've not seen much fun from you yet. You were more interested in the street names than getting to know me."

I grimaced, but forced a smile. "The night is still young."

He scowled and muttered something under his breath about me being too old for him anyway. The cheek of the man.

Harold strode ahead of us with Ruby on his arm. She glanced over her shoulder and winked at me. I had to play along. I didn't want to be pleasant to Richard, but I took his arm and kept the smile on my face as we walked towards what appeared to be a deserted building.

Harold knocked on the shabby entrance, and a few seconds later, a small sliding door about two-thirds of the way up opened. Harold muttered something, passed money through the entrance, and the bolt was slid, allowing us inside.

As soon as the door opened, I was hit with an unpleasant stench of sweaty bodies, alcohol, and cigarette smoke. I tightened my grip on Richard's arm.

"There's no need to worry. Most of the chaps in here are all bluster. Just watch out for the ones with bloody knuckles. They're the real fighters." He chortled to himself.

We walked along a poorly lit corridor, the crowd noise growing with every footstep. When we reached the entrance, I discovered at least three hundred people crammed into a single room. Harsh lights hung from the ceiling, and my attention was drawn to a boxing ring in the centre of the crowd. Everyone was talking, laughing, or drinking. The melee of noise was quite overwhelming.

"We won't be standing with this crowd, will we?" Ruby had to yell to be heard.

"There's an exclusive bit for us high rollers," Harold said. "It's roped off so the riff raff can't bother us. This way. Don't get lost in the crowd."

It took a fair amount of elbowing, stepping on feet, and shoving past people before we reached a quieter part of the venue. A burly looking man with no front teeth admitted us into a roped-off area, where we were served cheap champagne by a harried-looking waitress.

Harold settled into a seat and patted the spare one next to him for Ruby. "They'll be around soon to take our bets."

"Are we supposed to bet?" Ruby perched on the edge of the seat next to him. "I didn't bring much money."

"It's up to you, but it's part of the fun. My money is on the Russian."

"He's not Russian." Richard sat in a seat, and I had no choice but to sit next to him, unless I wanted to remain standing. "Polish. Possibly Greek. I never can understand the accents. Not English."

"Not many of them are. He's a killer," Harold said. "Covered in tattoos. He mainly grunts, though occasionally swears in his mother tongue. An absolute beast in the ring. You ladies are in for an eyeful tonight."

"We can't wait," Ruby said with forced cheeriness, although I spotted the worry in her eyes. I shared it. I hadn't expected there to be so many people.

Harold drained his glass of champagne and grimaced. "This is worse than warm dishwater. Richard, let's find some of the hard stuff."

"Are you leaving us?" Ruby asked.

"Don't worry your pretty little head. We won't be long at the bar. May I get you ladies anything?" Harold asked.

"No, thank you," I said.

The men left us with only the burly, missing-toothed man as our protector.

"While we have the chance, we should ask around about Arthur." I leaned close to Ruby so I could speak in her ear.

DEATH AT THE DRIPPING TAP 135

She looked at the crowd. "Where do we start?"

"With the other women." It took a few minutes, but I finally caught the harassed-looking waitress's eye and waved her over.

"More champagne?" Her words had an East End twang.

"We're looking for information about a fighter," I said.

"I can't give you insider hints about who to bet on. I just serve the drinks." She turned away.

I placed a healthy tip on her tray. "Arthur Blackstone. He used to box here."

She pocketed the money. "What about him? He's not fighting tonight. I haven't seen him for a few days."

"Did you ever see him get in trouble when he was here?"

"He used to beat his opponents to a pulp, so I doubt the other fighters liked him," she said.

"Was there anyone in particular he had a problem with? Someone who may have wanted to harm him?"

"This is a boxing club. The kind that runs at night. Everyone wants to harm someone in here. But the fighters sort their problems inside the ring." She glanced around the room. "I don't know what else to tell you."

"One last thing," I said. "Can you point out the man in charge?"

"Finn? He'll be at the back, talking to the fighters. He gives them a pep talk before they start, gets them geed up for when they step into the ring. He'll be out soon. You can't miss him. He's got a voice so loud he doesn't need a megaphone. I've got to go. Customers to serve." She dashed off.

"It seems word hasn't got around about Arthur's murder," I said to Ruby.

"Maybe they don't care he's dead," she said. "They must have people disappearing all the time once they've had enough of the fights. When they're no use to them, they pay no attention to what they do next."

"Let's speak to those ladies over there." I pointed through the crowd.

Ruby's eyes widened. "The ones sitting on the men's laps?"

"We can buy them a drink and say they need a five-minute break. Union rules. These girls must see everything, so we need to get them talking."

We pushed through the crowd until we arrived by the two unfortunate women. One of them noticed us and gave a big leery smile, although her eyes were devoid of kindness. "If you're looking for business, you're not dressed right."

"We're here from the Workers' Union for Ladies of Fallen Circumstances," I said. "It's time for your regulation break."

"Regulation what?" She nudged her friend. "Look at this. Apparently, we get to take a break."

"It's paid for, and you can come back once you're refreshed," I said.

"I'm staying here." Her friend didn't look amused by our intervention.

"Me too. Shove off, both of you. You're trying to steal our business, and we're having none of it. Don't make me chase you out of here. Finn lets us in, so we're allowed to work."

Ruby nudged me, and I followed her gaze to see a knife in the other woman's hand. We swiftly withdrew. After that unsuccessful attempt to gather information, we tried speaking to a few members of the crowd, but were met with hostility or ignored. Nobody wanted to talk, and the atmosphere grew increasingly unfriendly.

"It's time to place your final bets." A booming male voice made me jump, and I turned towards the ring. A huge man wearing a white vest under his open shirt strode around the ring as people cheered. "Ten minutes until the fights begin."

There was another roar of approval, and he slipped under the ring rope and walked away.

"That must be Finn! Let's follow him." I grabbed Ruby's hand, and we weaved, barged, and shoved our way through the crowd, finally getting to a door at the back. We slipped through, and I spotted Finn enter a room.

Ruby tugged on my arm. "Perhaps we should go back and find Harold and Richard."

"They won't be any use to us," I whispered. "They don't strike me as the fighting sort."

"But we could use them as a distraction in case we get into trouble," Ruby said.

"We just want to ask Finn a few questions about Arthur. If he turns nasty, we'll leave."

"What if he doesn't let us leave?"

I pressed a finger to my lips. We were almost at the room Finn had walked into. I peeked around the side of the door. Finn stood in front of twelve men, many of whom were dressed in vests and fighting shorts, or had their chests bared.

There was a crash behind me, and Ruby gasped. I turned to see she'd knocked over an empty bottle of wine someone had left in the corridor. It rolled across the uneven stone floor, chinking and rattling.

Before we could escape, the door was yanked open. Finn glared at us. "Well, well, well. What do we have here?"

Chapter 14

Since we'd been discovered, I blustered it out. "Good evening. Are you the man in charge of this fine establishment?"

Finn leered at me. "The last time I checked, I was. What are prim-looking ladies like you doing in a place like this?"

"We were invited to attend."

"My man on the door wouldn't have let you in, so you must have snuck in. What do you want?"

I refused to back down. "We paid to be here, the same as everybody else."

Finn's gaze ran over us, cold as a December day and just as bitter. "You must have come in with the posh lot." He grabbed us both by an arm, and we were yanked into the room. The door slammed shut.

I tried to pull my arm away from his grasp, but it was like battling with a vice, and his fingers wouldn't move. "We're not here for trouble, but we're looking for information about one of your fighters."

"Got you in the family way, has he?" Finn smirked, his gaze on my stomach.

"Nothing of the sort," I said. "We have a connection to Arthur Blackstone. We're aware he fought at this club."

"Don't know him. You're in the wrong place."

"Our sources are reliable."

"Sources! You sound like a copper." Finn reared back as if I'd slapped him. "Hold on a minute, you're not one of those newfangled women officers everyone is talking about? It's wrong, women forcing men to follow rules. How are you supposed to protect yourselves? How would you deal with the likes of us?"

Several of the men chuckled and cracked their knuckles.

"We don't work for the police," Ruby said. "But we do need information. And we're willing to pay, aren't we?"

I nodded. She meant I was willing to pay. And I was happy to part with money if it got us the information we needed and out of danger.

"No one will talk to you," Finn said. "We make a good living here, so there's no point in trying to bribe us. Although you could have something we need." His gaze ran over us again, causing my stomach to curdle.

"We're respectable ladies," Ruby said.

"Then you made a mistake by coming here," Finn said. "Look, boys. One of you will have a treat when this is over. How about the winner takes all?"

"How very dare you," I said.

Finn shoved his face close to mine. "I dare very much. You come into my place, demanding answers, and then try to bribe me. What did you think would happen?"

"We're here because a man has got himself into trouble. Do the decent thing and assist us," I said.

"I'll assist you all right." Finn grabbed Ruby and slung her over his shoulder, cheered on by the other men.

I stepped back, twisted, and thumped him with my handbag. Unfortunately, I had the ridiculously small, beaded bag Ruby insisted I bring, so it made barely any impact against his solid biceps.

Finn caught me by the back of my dress, causing it to tear, and dragged me through the room towards the other men. I kicked him hard in the shin, but he behaved as if he hadn't felt it. Was the man made of steel?

"You don't want me getting rough with you." Finn grunted as Ruby kicked him in the back. "Behave yourselves, and nobody has to be injured. Get that door open, lads. We'll let the ladies cool down in the cupboard."

One of the fighters opened the door to what looked like a cleaning cupboard. We were thrust inside, and the door slammed in our faces, plunging us into darkness as a key turned in the lock.

We thumped on the door for several seconds, but no one was eager to let us out.

"What a cheek," Ruby said. "He handled me as if I was a sack of potatoes. And he had his hand firmly on my behind."

"Never mind your bottom. We need to get out of here before the fights end, or we'll become playthings for those men."

"I agree. But this door is our only way out." She fiercely kicked the door several times.

I fumbled around in the hopes of finding a light switch, but there was none to be had. "Do you have matches?"

"Yes! Let me see if I can find them. They're always at the bottom of my bag." Ruby fumbled around in her handbag before pulling out a small box of matches. She struck one, giving us a few seconds of light to look around. It was an interior room, so there were no windows.

"How about that vent up by the ceiling? If it's big enough, we could wiggle through and get into another room." I hurried to the opposite wall and peered up at the small, rusted vent.

"Or we could find ourselves stuck and thoroughly embarrassed," Ruby said. "Someone must come to their senses and let us out before this situation gets out of hand."

"It's already out of hand. We won't get help from the men in that room," I said. "Not now we've been offered up as a prize."

"It's disgusting," Ruby said. "Finn must know he can't get away with this."

"Perhaps it's not the first time he's done it," I said. "And working girls are less likely to complain about bad treatment."

"I'll give him what for the next time he opens the door." Ruby lit another match, and we looked around for any other options to aid in our escape.

"Take this broom. It'll make a handy weapon."

The match died just as Ruby collected the broom from me. "How long do you think the fights will last?"

"I can't imagine they'll take more than a couple of hours. There are six fights, but if there's a knockout in the first round of each, this will be over soon."

"We need as much time as possible to figure our way out of this mess," Ruby said. "I wish Benji was here. He'd have bitten them all and sent them scurrying away like the naughty schoolboys they are."

"You're right. Finn wouldn't have dared come near us if Benji was by my side," I said. Although I was secretly glad Benji hadn't joined in this evening's adventure. He was a fearless dog, but every dog had his limits.

After several more matches and a few more minutes of searching, Ruby had a broom and a mallet, and I held a mop and a screwdriver. We wouldn't defeat a room full of fighters, but we'd be sure to land punishing blows, maybe making them think twice, and giving us a chance to escape.

A key jangled in the lock, making me tense. "Get ready. Someone must have come back early to sample their prize."

The door opened, and for a second, I was dazzled by the light. Even so, I thrust out the screwdriver. "Stay back. We're armed."

"You bleedin' idiot. Put that screwdriver down before you have an eye out."

My gaze focused, and I was surprised to see not a bare-chested fighter, but a burly woman standing in front of me. An angry, burly woman.

"Who are you?" I asked.

"I'm here to get you out. Come on." She ushered us out of the cleaning cupboard with an irritated wave.

"How did you know we were in here?" Ruby asked.

"I overheard some of the men joking about the totty who visited them. I knew what they were talking about, and what they had planned for you." The woman glowered at us. "A bare-knuckle fight club is no place for ladies. I don't know how you got in here, but you must have expected trouble."

"We're not here for any kind of trouble," I said. "Why are you here if it's such an unsuitable place for a woman?"

"This is a family business." She glared at us. "And the only type of woman who should be here are those who have business to conduct, if you get my meaning."

"We met some of them," I said. "They weren't terribly helpful."

"Why would they be? They probably thought you were muscling in on their trade." Her expression turned puzzled. "I suppose there must be men who like that look."

"I'll have you know, this is last season's finest," Ruby said.

"Whatever it is, I don't care. Follow me. I'll take you out the back and you can be on your way." The woman turned and strode off. "Keep up."

We kept hold of our weapons as we hurried out of the now empty room and turned right out of the door, following our mystery rescuer.

"What's your name?" I asked.

"None of your business."

"I'd like to thank you."

She sighed. "Jenny."

"Thank you for your help, Jenny. We were struggling to find a solution to our imprisonment."

"You're not in the clear yet. Hurry, and be quiet."

I lowered my voice. "You said this business was a family concern?"

She nodded in response.

"Jenny! What are you doing? And why are you with those two?" A man stepped out of another room, blocking our path.

"I'm making sure Finn doesn't do something he'll regret." Jenny kept walking.

"He said he had two women for the lads. I thought—"

Jenny clocked him squarely on the jaw with a large fist, sending him sprawling unconscious to the floor. "Keep moving! He'll be down for a while, but once he's on his feet, he'll tell Finn what's going on."

"Goodness! You can throw a smashing punch," Ruby said.

"As I mentioned, this is a family business. I've been in the ring a few times, so I know what I'm doing."

"I can see that," I said. "And thank you again for getting us out of that cupboard."

Jenny glanced over her shoulder at me. "It looked like you were prepared to fight. But don't get yourselves mixed up with this bunch. If you spend any time here, you'll get a reputation you can't come back from."

"Do you work here?" I asked.

"My cousin runs this place. Finn. I keep order with the ladies. Watch out for trouble. When I heard what you two were up to, I knew you were the kind of trouble that needed dealing with."

"We were only looking for answers," I said.

Jenny stopped by a back door, a hand resting on it. "Answers about what?"

"One of the fighters who used to come here," I said. "Arthur Blackstone. Do you know him?"

Her eyes narrowed. "Of course. What do you want to know about him?"

"Everything! Well, I don't know if you're aware, but Arthur died recently."

Jenny gulped. "I heard a rumour something bad happened to him. I'm not surprised. He was the definition of trouble. Knew his way around the ring, though. He was going places, getting a reputation as a fighter not to be messed with. Finn was talking about giving him a weekly slot on the circuit."

"How did you find out he died?" Ruby asked.

"People gossip. I wasn't certain, but I heard there was a fight at a pub. Is that right?"

"Arthur was found outside the Dripping Tap," I said. "He was attacked on the street."

Jenny sighed. "You'd think a fighter would be able to protect himself. Nowhere is safe these days."

"Did you know him well?" I asked.

"I keep to myself. It's the best way to be when you work in a place like this," Jenny said. "But I notice the ones who are great in the ring. They always pose and preen as if they're God's gift to women. And they get a lot of attention from the ladies. Some nonsense about liking a bad boy. All clap-trap if you ask me. The best thing a woman can do is learn how to protect herself." She eyed the screwdriver I still held.

"I couldn't agree more," I said.

"And make sensible choices, such as not coming to an illegal bare-knuckle fight club on their own and expect to get away with it," Jenny said. "I'll be having a word with Bongo on the door. He knows better than to let you in. Although the man was born with cotton wool for a brain."

"We didn't come here alone," Ruby said. "Two male friends escorted us in."

"Then they're as stupid as you are. And where are these friends now? Abandoned you once you got in trouble with Finn." Jenny shook her head. "These blokes, they're all the same. Get what they want and then leave."

"Was Arthur like that?" I asked.

"I couldn't tell you. I watched him fight, and that's it."

"What about any problems he had with fellow boxers?" I asked. "Or any trouble with a romantic relationship?"

"We weren't friends. If Arthur was unhappy with someone, they slugged it out in the ring. He had a temper and used it to his advantage. A lot of the other fighters were scared of him."

"That could have made Finn wealthy," I said. "He had a potential prize fighter working for him."

"Finn makes decent money off all the fights, but he has his favourites. Now, you need to get out of here." She shoved open the door to reveal a dank, unpleasant-smelling alleyway. "Turn left and walk to the end. That'll get you onto the street. But don't hang around. The outside is almost as bad as the inside."

"I work at the London Times," I said. "If you can think of any useful information about Arthur's enemies or trouble he'd got himself into recently, you can contact me there. I'm Veronica Vale."

"Why? You poking about for a story?"

"No, but I'm concerned the police have the wrong man for Arthur's murder," I said. "The landlord of the Dripping Tap is the prime suspect, but I'm sure it wasn't him. I'm investigating what actually happened to Arthur."

Jenny's eyebrows rose, but she didn't respond.

"We need to know everything about Arthur to find more credible suspects," Ruby said. "If you have information, it would be ever so helpful. An innocent man can't go down for a crime he didn't commit."

"I'll think on it, but like I said, I didn't know him. I'm sorry if someone else is getting in trouble for this when they don't deserve it, but it's not my business. It shouldn't be your business either." Jenny's head jerked up, and her eyes narrowed. "That's a police siren! Someone called the old bill on us. Get out of here." She shoved us into the alleyway and slammed the door.

I grabbed Ruby's hand as we skirted soggy boxes and empty pallets, heading towards the main street.

"It sounds like Arthur had a reputation as a ruthless fighter," Ruby said.

"And that put a target on his back," I said. "I don't think Finn's a suspect, though. After all, if Arthur was making him money, he wouldn't want him out of commission."

"Perhaps Arthur decided he no longer wanted to fight," Ruby said. "They argued, and Finn attacked him."

The sirens were getting ever closer. And there was more than one.

"When we get back to yours, I'm having a big cup of hot cocoa and a pile of toast," Ruby said. "After all this excitement, I need to settle my nerves. My heart is racing."

"You sound like my mother," I teased. We reached the end of the alleyway, and I poked my head out. "There are four police cars and a dozen officers. We need to make a run for it. We don't want to get caught here. And they'll search this alley, so we have little time."

"We'll behave as if we're out for an evening stroll," Ruby said. "They won't look at us twice. They're after drunken men at a fight club, not two respectable ladies."

"On three," I said and counted down on my fingers.

We brazened it out, stepping onto the street, and headed away from the police cars, arm in arm and chins up, behaving as if we had every right to be there.

"Hey! Stop right there."

Drat. Caught again.

Chapter 15

I'd had a remarkably good sleep, considering I'd spent the night in a small cell at a police station. After our unsuccessful attempt to flee the fight, we'd been arrested, processed, and detained for questioning.

Perhaps my pleasant sleep was because the officers took pity on me and Ruby and put us in their more luxurious cells. The mattress had been firm, if a little thin, and the room cold, but I preferred a cool room to sleep in, so it hadn't been a hardship.

However, the confinement was wearing on me. I'd called an officer several times to find out what was going on, but he said they had bigger priorities than two ladies of the night, and they'd get around to us when they could. I was unsure whether to be amused or irritated by the possibility I'd been mistaken as a lady who sold those particular services. As a more mature woman, I wasn't sure there'd be a market for providing such an offering, but perhaps I was mistaken.

Although my unexpected stay in the police cell hadn't been unpleasant, I was growing concerned. I'd heard nothing about Ruby, and I could only imagine the state my mother had worked herself into when we hadn't returned home. She'd have had Matthew ringing the hospitals to find out if we'd been involved in some terrible tragedy. I'd considered telephoning home, but I couldn't think of a convenient reason why Ruby and I had been out all night.

I stretched, gently working the kinks out of my spine, and shuffled my feet into my shoes. I had to face the music. My family would find out where we'd been, but perhaps once we found Arthur's killer, there'd be less scolding.

The door to the cell opened, and a police officer who was at least eight years my junior stepped inside with a tray containing toast and a cup of tea. "Breakfast, and then we'll be ready for you."

"What am I to prepare myself for?" I asked.

"Questions. We've been busy all night, dealing with the illegal goings on we discovered you running away from."

"I wasn't running. It was a swift walk. Did you make many arrests? I imagine the men who organise such activities are used to absconding efficiently, so they'd be tricky to stop."

"We got enough of them. And the ones talking are telling us the same names. I'm sure you'll do likewise. You are going to cooperate, aren't you?"

"It depends on how stewed my tea is," I said.

"You behave yourself, and you should get off with a warning." He set down the tray and stepped back. "It makes me sad to see you older types down on your luck and selling the only thing you've got left."

My mouth fell open. Then I laughed. "You think I sell lascivious services?"

"Lascivious what?"

"Selling the only thing I have left. My ample charms." Although I was hardly ample. Ruby filled her curves, but I was always striding about, burning up energy as fast as I consumed it to be anything other than a waspish shadow.

"It's becoming more common," the officer said. "People blame the war. Some of you ladies took on the men's jobs, but when they came home, you had to give them back. You were earning a few bob, and you didn't want to stop."

"And of course, I have no other services or skills to offer other than to flirt with a man?"

The young officer blushed. "That's not for me to say."

"I should demand an apology," I said. "But I find the whole situation amusing."

"You won't find it amusing if you're charged with soliciting."

"I assure you, I won't be. My details were taken down, and I was processed before being brought into the cell. The pieces must have been put together by now." I took a sip of the tea. It was hot and well brewed, if a little strong for my taste.

"Like I said, it's been a busy night. We're shorthanded after that business with the bomb over in the slums. We're doing what we can, but..." he gave a small shrug and tugged at his starched collar.

"My apologies. I'm aware of the troubles you've had. I know Inspector Jacob Templeton."

The officer startled. "Is he one of your clients?"

"Don't be ridiculous. Spend five minutes learning about who I am, and you'll understand my connection to this place. I've been most useful to the police. And I can be useful again, but my progress remains stuck while I'm here."

"That's not for me to get involved with. Someone will be by shortly to take you to the interview room." He turned to leave.

"Before you go, may I ask about my companion, Ruby Smythe? We were brought in together. I asked the officer who was here overnight, but he told me nothing."

"Oh! She's the pretty one with the dark hair?"

"Yes, she is remarkably pretty. Did you ask her about selling services as a more mature woman, too?"

He blustered some nonsense words, growing redder by the second. "She told me about her work with horses. I wasn't sure I believed her, but she knew her stuff."

"Ruby sounds in fine spirits," I said. "She likes her toast barely brown if you haven't yet served her."

"I'll see what I can do." His blush deepened, and it was clear Ruby had had an impact on this young man.

I finished my tea and ate my toast while I waited for someone to collect me. Almost half an hour passed before the door was unlocked again. Sergeant Matthers appeared. A very grumpy, hurriedly dressed-looking Sergeant Matthers. "Miss Vale! I just got word you and Ruby were in the cells after being arrested at a fight. The boys think you were selling your ... services. Please tell me it's not true."

"Which part?"

He stepped into the cell and closed the door behind him. "Inspector Templeton was worried you'd do something like this. He told me to keep an eye on you, and now this has happened. I'll lose my job!"

"I assure you, you won't. If trouble comes your way, I'll speak up for you. You had nothing to do with this. You told us repeatedly not to get involved, but we didn't listen. Blame us for being foolish females if it gets you off the hook."

He sighed and massaged his forehead with the tips of his fingers. "Why did the other officers think you and Ruby were selling your services at the club?"

"Wishful thinking? It's an idea that appears to have lodged in their heads," I said. "I'll admit, we were dressed in a most becoming fashion, but we were attempting to leave the venue when the police raid occurred. They didn't find us in a compromising position."

"I suppose to some fellows, that's the only thing that makes sense—to have a woman in such a place. We arrested a few other ladies as well. They're known to us. Regulars in the cells. Sometimes, I pick them up just to give them a night off and a safe bed."

"That's decent of you," I said.

He inclined his head. "What were you and Ruby doing there? Or do I already know the answer to that question?"

"You are as astute as you are kind. We'd hoped to speak to the man in charge about Arthur. We attempted several conversations with other guests, but they weren't willing to talk."

"Of course they wouldn't!" He massaged his forehead so hard, I could only assume something had given him a headache. "Did you find out anything useful?"

"Not a jot. We hoped to have a quiet word with Finn, the owner, but regrettably, we were discovered snooping. He was most ungentlemanly, and we ended up locked in a cupboard."

Sergeant Matthers's face paled. "You were fortunate that's all that happened."

"It's not just fortune. We had an ally. A woman named Jenny works at the club. She's Finn's cousin."

"I know Jenny. And Finn. Finn Grey. They've been in the business for years," Sergeant Matthers said. "Sneaky types. I can never pin anything on them."

"They weren't arrested last night?"

"They both got away. They always do. Finn has lookouts posted close to the club, so he gets word when a raid is coming. I wouldn't be surprised if he doesn't bribe a few officers to make sure he gets inside information about when we're planning a visit."

"Jenny was quick to throw us out and race back inside. She must have gone to help Finn get away."

"She's always been loyal to the family," Sergeant Matthers said. "But she's already been spoken to in relation to Arthur's death."

"She didn't know much about Arthur," I said. "When we spoke to her, she'd heard rumours that he'd got himself in trouble, but wasn't sure he was dead."

"Then she didn't tell you the truth. Jenny and Arthur were in a relationship. Apparently, it wasn't long-term, and things came to a natural end, so there were no hard feelings between them."

"How peculiar. Why would she say she knew nothing about him or his murder when you'd already interviewed her? You did tell her he was dead?"

"We did. Perhaps she doesn't like strangers poking about in her private business," Sergeant Matthers said.

"You snuck in somewhere you shouldn't have been and expected everyone to open their arms and welcome you while telling you all their secrets. You know better than that, Miss Vale."

"Perhaps I was naïve." I rested on the bed and swung my legs. "This case is perplexing. Whichever way we turn, we find no suitable suspects to ensure Stanley's innocence."

"Could that be because he's guilty?" Sergeant Matthers said. "You must admit, you don't know the fellow well. I understand you want to protect your employee, but sometimes, the simplest path is the right one."

I sighed. "I'm not giving up just yet. How's Ruby?"

"Having the time of her life. You'd think we'd sent her to Blackpool for a seaside holiday, not put her in a prison cell." Sergeant Matthers chuckled as he shook his head. "She's had the officers eating out of her hand. They brought her extra food, blankets, and pillows. When I looked in on her, she was tucked in bed snoring."

"Don't say you heard her snoring. She hates it when anyone mentions that unbecoming trait," I cautioned with a wry smile.

He grinned. "Nothing phases her. You could probably put her in a prisoner of war camp, and she'd thrive."

My smile faded a fraction. Ruby had been through difficult times during the Great War. She'd shared the information with me only once, and I'd promised to keep it to myself, but those hard times ensured she fought hard to find the joy in every situation.

"What happens now?" I asked. "The officer who brought me breakfast said I'd be interviewed."

"You're free to go," Sergeant Matthers said. "I've cleared everything with the other officer and explained who you are."

"Thank goodness. I'm not sure I'm ready to be tarred and feathered just yet."

"The next time you go on a daring adventure, let me know, so I can stop any risk of tarring and feathering."

"You're adorable for looking out for us, but that's why we kept you out of the loop," I said.

"I'd have talked sense into you. Charging into a place like that and expecting to come out all sunshine and roses. Whatever next?"

"Perhaps we overstretched a fraction," I said. "Can we keep this little inconvenience between us? If Inspector Templeton finds out, it could set back his recovery." And lead to me getting a sharp earful about irresponsible behaviour.

"I won't lie to the inspector," Sergeant Matthers said, "but if he doesn't ask, I won't say anything."

"You're an angel," I said.

"I'll go and see how Ruby is doing. The paperwork is already processed, so you'll be out of here soon. I imagine you want to go home and rest."

"I need to get to work," I said. "If we're quick, I won't be late. Thank you, Sergeant Matthers. You've been an absolute rock."

"Don't let it happen again," he said.

I made no promises. I couldn't. After all, when there was a murder to investigate, one sometimes engaged in mildly dangerous activities to ensure a successful result.

A mere ten minutes later, we had our possessions returned to us, and I stood outside the police station, blinking in the bright morning sunshine with Ruby beside me.

"What an absolute hoot," she said. "Not only are we crime-fighters, but we're also criminals."

"Criminal crime-fighters who need a suitable excuse for why we didn't return home last night." I hailed a taxi. We climbed in, and I gave the address for home.

"Oh dear. I hadn't thought about that." Ruby bit her lip. "Perhaps we could say we were out so late that we didn't want to disturb your mother and Matthew, so we stayed in a hotel."

"I'm considering coming clean," I said.

"Your mother's heart won't stand for it!"

"I'll make her see sense. We can't have one of our landlords involved in a murder investigation. This is for the greater good."

"Perhaps I won't come back with you," Ruby said. "I don't want to be shouted at."

"I'll take the brunt of the shouting," I said. "You stand behind me."

We arrived home, and I paid the taxi driver and climbed out. I inched open the front door and peered into the hallway. It seemed silent. I gestured for Ruby to follow me, and we crept into the hallway, quickly taking off our fancy shoes and jackets.

Matthew appeared in the kitchen doorway. He stared at us for a few seconds and then gestured us over with his finger. We walked into the kitchen, and he closed the door behind us. "Where have you been?"

"It's a long story. The summary is, we followed a lead on a murder suspect and ended up getting arrested," I said.

His eyebrows rose. "For what?"

"Selling our unique services," Ruby said with a little shimmy. "Can you imagine?"

His forehead furrowed, then his eyebrows shot up again. "That's preposterous."

Ruby pouted.

"How angry is Mother?" I asked.

"She slept through the night. Me, on the other hand, I've been pacing my room wondering what was going on."

I hugged him. He was an absolute dear. "Thank you for worrying, but there was no need. Mother really knows nothing about this?"

"I'm tempted to tell on you. You had me worried half to death." He pulled away from my hug and paced across the kitchen, filling the kettle and setting it on the hob. "You smell of cigarette smoke."

"There were no washing facilities in the police station," I said. "I'll tell you everything later. But we have no time to dally. We need a quick wash, change, and then we're visiting Jenny."

"Whatever for?" Ruby was already rummaging in the pantry for food, despite being fed at the police station.

I politely ignored Matthew's grumbled protests. "She lied about not knowing Arthur, and I'm determined to find out why."

Chapter 16

After more scolding from Matthew and taking five minutes to freshen up, I made use of Uncle Harry's endless connections to discover where Jenny lived.

"From your description, Crawshaw Farm sounds like an arable farm," I said to him, the telephone connection crackling in my ear. "Is that over the border into Essex?"

"That's right. Jenny's family must have relocated out of London because of the dangers during the Great War," Uncle Harry said. "According to my source, Jenny helps run the family farm, along with her mother and brother."

"While having an interesting sideline in evening activities," I said.

"Farmers can struggle to make ends meet," Uncle Harry said. "I take it you'll investigate this right away?"

"I know I'm taking a liberty, but could I have the morning off? I'll make it up to you. I'll stay late."

"Take all the time you need. Although, of course, Bob is asking where you are. I said it's a family matter and he should keep his nose out, unless he wants to write a piece about the sewer blockages on Westwell Road."

"Thank you. I appreciate it. There's something going on with Jenny. She lied to my face about knowing Arthur. Why do that unless she has something to hide?"

"Stay safe. And I'm trying hard not to believe the rumours about you and Ruby getting locked up last night, but you've made me worry."

"Even if we were locked up, and I'm not confirming we were, we're free now, and I must get to the bottom of what happened to Arthur."

We said our goodbyes. I peeked in on my mother, who was remarkably still asleep, and then dashed out of the house with Ruby, Benji happily back by my side. Once Ruby had filled up with petrol and we'd checked the directions to Crawshaw Farm, we were on our way.

Ruby had brought snacks for the journey, pilfered from my mother's pantry, and I was keeping an eye on the map to ensure we stayed on course. It was rare we ventured out of London together, so this felt like a holiday.

The busy London streets gave way to quieter roads, and soon country lanes dominated, where the only other traffic was belching tractors and bleating sheep.

I wound down the window and breathed in the fresh air. "Once you've been inside a prison cell, things seem different."

"We've experienced the brutality of having our freedom taken," Ruby said. "That changes a woman."

"I doubt you even noticed, given the extra supplies you were provided with. How many of the officers fell in love with you?"

She chortled. "Enough to ensure my stay was luxurious. Look out for a sign for the farm. We must be close."

I gripped my seat. Ruby loved to push her car to its limits, and even whizzing along these narrow country lanes, she didn't take her foot off the gas pedal.

"Slow down a jot. I can barely see straight," I said.

"This looks like it." The back wheels of the car skidded as Ruby took a sharp left turn. She slowed as we passed open fields full of crops.

"There's a building up ahead," I said. "It could be the farmhouse."

As we rounded the corner, a large detached building with a tiled roof and several barns close by appeared.

"Find a spot to tuck the car away," I said. "We'll watch to see if anybody's home."

We only had to wait a few moments before a tractor trundled into view and parked next to a large, open-backed truck. A young man came out of the farmhouse, and a second later, Jenny followed. They started hauling bales of hay off the truck and onto the ground.

Jenny worked for several minutes before resting. She turned, knuckling her fingers into the small of her back, then settled a hand on her stomach. Since she stood in profile to us, I immediately saw her situation. "Oh dear. I think Arthur didn't only abandon Jenny when their relationship ended."

Before Ruby could respond to confirm my suspicions, Jenny turned her head, squinting straight at us, then marched over.

"What do we do?" Ruby asked.

"We can hardly run," I said. "We'll brazen it out. I'll give an excuse for why we're visiting."

"What are you doing here?" Jenny stopped by the car, a scowl on her face. "I thought the old bill had you."

"They understood their mistake and let us go," I said. "We stopped by to thank you for helping last night. We found ourselves in a difficult situation, which would have been much worse if you hadn't let us out of that cupboard."

Jenny's scowl remained in place. "How do you know where I live? Get off our land. I knew you were trouble when I saw you at the club. And now you're here. You'd better not have told the police about me." Her hands fisted.

"They have nothing on you or your cousin," I said.

She grunted. "Nor will they. Finn runs a slick operation."

"Jenny! Jenny! I almost caught one." The young man who'd been helping unload the straw ran over, his jumper covered in pale animal fur and the knees of his trousers muddy.

"Stop chasing those rabbits. I've already told you, you can't trap a wild rabbit and expect it to become tame. It'll never be friendly with you." Jenny affectionately rumpled the young man's hair. He was around eighteen. Tall, gangly, and full of smiles.

"He looked like Floppy. Maybe it was him." He gave her a beaming grin, full of innocence and excitement. "You said he'd come back. You told me he would if I did good."

Jenny sighed. "I think Floppy has hopped off to pastures new."

He frowned. "You said he would come back."

"Do you like animals?" I asked him.

The young man turned to me and nodded enthusiastically. His gaze darted over my shoulder as he spotted Benji. "He's yours?"

"He is. And he loves to make new friends. His name is Benji. Would you like to shake his paw?"

"We don't have time for this," Jenny said. "The hay needs unloading, and the horses feeding."

"Look at the dog! Can I stroke him?" The young man bounced on his toes, his eyes alight with pleasure.

Benji put on his best performance, gently whining and lifting one paw to look utterly irresistible. I reached back and opened the door so he could jump out and greet the young man.

He fell to his knees, engrossed in stroking Benji's fur. There was a similarity in features between the young fellow and Jenny, so I had to assume they were related. "Is this your brother?"

She nodded. "Gregory. He helps on the farm when he's not chasing local wildlife and trying to befriend it."

"I love animals too," I said to Gregory. "Dogs in particular. I volunteer at a charity that helps stray dogs. We even have a few cats and the occasional rabbit stay with us."

"Rabbits! They're my absolute favourite. I like dogs too, but I've always had rabbits."

I eased open my door and climbed out. Ruby followed me. "I get pleasure from making sure unwanted animals get good homes. Perhaps you'd like to visit the dogs' home with your sister and find a new rabbit to take care of?"

Gregory leapt up and hugged me so tightly I squeaked.

"Leave her alone," Jenny scolded. "Sorry, he gets excited when anyone pays him attention. Gregory, go inside. Ma might need you for something."

"Can we see the rabbits?" he asked her. "Mine are coming back soon, but I can't find them. Jenny promised they would, but they haven't."

"It would be no trouble to welcome you both to the dogs' home," I said. "We take in all sorts of strays. We once had fifty guinea pigs. Imagine that. The owner thought she had two girls, and unfortunately, one was a male. Things got out of control."

"We'll see about a visit," Jenny said.

"Please!" Gregory grabbed her hand. "I miss my rabbits. They were my friends."

"Let me think about it," Jenny said. "Go inside. There's work around the farmhouse that needs doing."

He jiggled from foot to foot for a few seconds before running off into the house.

"I hope you don't mind me saying this," Ruby said, "but perhaps in your condition, you shouldn't be hauling heavy bales of hay around."

Jenny's nostrils flared and her fingers flexed. "My condition?"

Ruby gulped, her gaze on Jenny's stomach. "We couldn't help but notice—"

Jenny lunged at Ruby, grabbing her around the throat and almost pulling her off her feet.

Benji jumped up, ramming his paws against Jenny's arm and barking fiercely.

"Keep quiet," Jenny hissed into Ruby's face. "My condition is none of your business."

"Whatever's going on out here?" A broad-shouldered surly woman with a floured apron wrapped around her middle ran out of the farmhouse with a rolling pin in one hand. "Jenny, let go of that woman."

"She's saying things she shouldn't," Jenny yelled, still holding onto Ruby's throat.

"Sorry," Ruby choked out. "I didn't want you doing any harm to the baby."

"Let her go, or I'll whack you into next week." Although the woman brandished the rolling pin, she made no move to strike Jenny.

Jenny huffed out her disgust and finally let go of Ruby, shoving her away, and glowering at Benji, who continued to bark. "I don't even know what they're doing here. These are the two I told you about who were at the club last night. They got themselves in trouble with Finn."

"Everybody calm down," the woman said. "My daughter is hotheaded, but she doesn't mean anything by it."

"Mrs Crawshaw?" I arched my eyebrows.

"That's right. This is my farm. And you're trespassing, so you'd better have a good reason for being here."

"We came to thank Jenny for getting us out of a tricky situation," I said.

"I know all about your tricky situation." Mrs Crawshaw speared Jenny with a sharp look that kept her quiet. "Foolish girls going to a place like that on your own."

Ruby cleared her throat. "We had gentlemen friends with us, but they abandoned us."

"Then they were hardly gentlemen," Mrs Crawshaw said. "I'm sorry about Jenny. She didn't mean it. Do you need anything for your throat? Jenny boxes and sometimes forgets her own strength."

"I startled her," Ruby said. "I'll be fine. I've come through worse scrapes unharmed."

"If you say so."

We all stared at each other.

"Is it Arthur's baby?" I boldly asked Jenny.

"Do you see now why I choked that one?" Jenny said to her mother. "They won't stop asking questions that have nothing to do with them."

"Not because we're nosy," I said. "I own the pub close to where Arthur's body was found. My landlord, a very capable man, is about to be charged with Arthur's murder. I believe he's innocent, so I must make sure the right man is found and appropriately punished."

"And as I told you last night, I didn't know Arthur," Jenny said.

"That's not the truth, is it?" I persisted. "I discovered you had a romantic relationship with him."

"That's no secret," Mrs Crawshaw said. "Why didn't you tell them?"

"Because it's none of their business," Jenny said. "And I didn't want my name getting dragged into things. I said I didn't know Arthur because I hoped they'd leave me alone. I told the police everything, and that was the end of it. Then these two appear in Finn's club and rake things up. It got me angry."

"But this is Arthur's baby?" I asked again.

Jenny glowered at me, but eventually nodded. "I'm raising it myself. And I have my family around to help me. The baby will want for nothing."

"And we're happy to do so," Mrs Crawshaw said. "This won't be the first child out of wedlock this family has dealt with. And I'll welcome my first grandbaby into the world."

"You told the police the relationship came to a natural end. Surely, if there's a baby involved, Arthur would have proposed marriage," I said. And if he'd abandoned Jenny after learning about the pregnancy, it gave her a perfect motive for wanting him dead.

"Jenny was never interested in Arthur as a husband," Mrs Crawshaw said. "We don't need a useless man around to raise a child."

Jenny nodded. "Neither of us wanted to marry. We liked each other's company, but it wasn't love. Why would I saddle myself with a man I didn't love? He was fun to spend time with now and again, and we were always careful, although clearly not careful enough." She settled a hand on her belly. "I told him about the baby, and he asked if we should marry, but I said no. I can look after myself just fine. That was when we ended things. The farm was getting busy, and with a baby on the way, I had no time for him."

"How did Arthur take the news?" Ruby asked.

"He seemed surprised, but took it in his stride. We parted as friends."

"And now Arthur is dead," I said. "Murdered."

"He ran with some dangerous people," Jenny said. "It was another reason not to keep him around. I couldn't risk someone like that being close to my baby."

It was also another reason to kill him. Mothers go to extraordinary lengths to protect their children. "May I ask where you were when Arthur was attacked?"

"The police know that information. I don't need to tell you," Jenny said.

"You've told most of your secrets. Why not this bit of news?" Mrs Crawshaw asked. "If you don't, I will, since it won't cause a problem."

I turned to her. "Do you know where Jenny was at the time of the murder?"

"She was here. We were up late that night because a horse was foaling. All three of us stayed up to make sure everything went well." Mrs Crawshaw gestured over her shoulder with a thumb. "If you're asking if she was fighting with Arthur that night, then no, because we were together. You can see the foal for yourself. Adorable little thing. Gregory is obsessed with it. Almost as obsessed as he was with those rabbits."

"Could we confirm that with Gregory?" I asked.

"You cheeky—" Jenny stepped forward, but her mother blocked her and yelled for Gregory, who bounded out of the house like an eager puppy.

"What did you tell the police about your sister?" she asked him.

He pointed at the barn. "We've got a baby horse. A foal! We were helping with it."

"Now you can leave," Jenny said. "And don't come back asking more nosy questions. I've told the police all I know, and I'm done talking to a pair of busybody troublemakers."

I glanced at Ruby, and she nodded. We swiftly said our goodbyes and returned to the car with Benji.

We settled in and Ruby pulled away. "What do you think?"

"Jenny has excellent motives." My heart was beating a little too fast after that encounter.

"But a good alibi. Her mother and brother confirming her whereabouts is a problem."

"Yes, that's a pity."

"Jenny is strong, though, and she has a temper." Ruby turned onto the single-lane road.

"As you discovered. The police don't seem interested in her. Sergeant Matthers dismissed her as a suspect almost immediately." I looked at Ruby. "How does your throat feel?"

"Sore. I'll bruise." She blew out a breath.

"Could her mother be lying to protect her?" I suggested.

"Maybe. But Gregory, too? He seems a simple sort. Not the kind to be capable of lying."

I nodded. "He does. I doubt he'd be comfortable keeping such a huge secret."

Ruby sped along the country lane. "Gosh. After the fight club, prison, and Jenny almost strangling me to death, I need a cold compress and a stiff gin."

I huffed a laugh. "Don't we all?"

Chapter 17

"You've barely touched your evening meal. Do you need me to cut the sausage into smaller pieces so it's easier to eat? I must admit, they look gristly." I made a move to take Inspector Templeton's knife, but he snatched it away.

"I'm not a child! How many times do I need to tell you to stop fussing over me?"

"My calculations suggest at least a thousand." That comment earned me the smallest of smiles. Ever since I'd arrived at the hospital that evening with Ruby, Inspector Templeton's mood had been acerbic, and his tone snappy.

"You need to keep your strength up," Ruby said. "Once you get out of here, there'll be a mountain of work for you to catch up on."

"And most likely, everything Detective Chief Inspector Taylor has touched will need reviewing," I said. "I don't trust that man."

"He's not that bad," Inspector Templeton said. "Although he has been pushing me to get back to work as soon as possible. I get the impression he's forgotten what a hard day's work feels like."

"He's more used to days on the golf course and fine dining with influential types than rolling up his sleeves and helping people." I gestured for Inspector Templeton to continue eating, but he shook his head. He glanced at Ruby and the artfully tied scarf she had around her neck. "Are you going to tell me about the trouble you've been getting into?"

"No trouble." I moved his food out of the way and settled on the end of the bed. "The case is overdue a breakthrough, though. It's jolly frustrating how little progress we've made."

"From what I hear, Stanley is still the prime suspect," Inspector Templeton said. "That's progress."

I tutted. "Then you are out of the loop. We've been exploring other avenues."

"But you've yet to find the killer," Inspector Templeton said. "Is that because he's already behind bars, and you've been putting yourselves in danger and wasting time for no reason?"

"Untrue. Arthur's brother, Ernie, could be the killer. Sergeant Matthers is checking his alibi."

"And there's also Patrick, Arthur's illegal lodger who we caught red-handed," Ruby said.

"He's been ruled out," Inspector Templeton said. "Given members of my team saw him in a different location at the time Arthur was killed, it couldn't have been him."

"Perhaps they made a mistake," I said. "It was very late. They must have been tired. Eyes play tricks on the weary."

"They didn't make a mistake. Arthur was well known to us."

"Finn, the owner of the illegal fighting ring, is another possibility." I slid a glance at Inspector Templeton, careful not to say too much in case it gave away our recent brush with danger. "The police have yet to find him or check his alibi."

"And we have Jenny Crawshaw, Arthur's former lady friend. Pregnant lady friend," Ruby said.

"That was a surprise," Inspector Templeton said. "I didn't know Arthur was to be a father."

"Jenny has an alibi, though," I said. "It's a wretched shame. When we spoke to her, she seemed the perfect fit. Angry, admitted she knows how to throw a punch—"

"Which we saw for ourselves," Ruby said.

I swiftly shook my head.

Ruby gasped. "I mean, I imagine she can. She said she could. And she's got huge hands."

"Let's go back a few steps, shall we?" Inspector Templeton said. "Firstly, how did you know Finn Grey heads up this illegal fighting institution?"

I glanced at Ruby. "We know how to do our research."

"Sergeant Matthers mentioned him," Ruby said.

He grunted. "And how do you know Jenny can throw a punch?"

"She said so!" Ruby said. "And her work must keep her fit."

"When was that?" Inspector Templeton asked.

"When was what?" I smoothed my skirt and looked around the room.

"Don't be obtuse."

Ruby adjusted her scarf. "It must have been when we interviewed her."

"And where did you interview her?"

"We've already told you we visited her family farm," I said. Inspector Templeton had received a blow-by-blow account of our recent adventures while he'd toyed with his gristly sausage and mashed potato.

"Jenny willingly revealed she boxes?" Inspector Templeton shook his head. "Why would she do that?"

"She told us she was Finn's cousin and helped at the fights," I said. "Perhaps she's proud of the fact she knows how to look after herself."

"If I could throw a punch like that, I would be," Ruby said.

Inspector Templeton grumbled to himself as he shifted in the bed. "This is too dangerous for you to be involved in."

"We've been in barely any danger," I said.

Inspector Templeton's expression darkened. "Sergeant Matthers told me everything. You and Ruby got into Finn's illegal boxing match."

"That sneak! He said he wouldn't tell," I said.

"I ordered him to. He was behaving oddly during his last visit. He kept stumbling over his words, and going red in the face. Sergeant Matthers is a terrible liar, so I knew he was hiding something. When I learned what it was, I was tempted to drag myself out of this bed and arrest you both. What you did was foolhardy. You could have been grievously injured."

"We were taking care of things," I said. "Perhaps we got in over our heads by visiting the club, but Jenny helped."

"She knocked a man out!" Ruby said. "It was ever so impressive."

There was a tap on the door, and Sergeant Matthers appeared. He stopped when he saw we were there. "I didn't think you'd have company so late, sir. I just finished my shift and wanted to check in."

"I suspect your ears are burning," I said. "We've just learned Inspector Templeton knows everything about our recent evening activities."

"Ah! Sorry, ladies, but I never disobey orders."

"Come in, Sergeant," Inspector Templeton said. "We were going over the suspects, and I was telling Veronica and Ruby to stop meddling before they come to serious harm."

Sergeant Matthers closed the door behind him and walked to the bed. "I warned them to be careful, but I had no success in stopping them."

"That's in the past," I said. "We're here now, and unharmed."

"Why is Ruby wearing that scarf?" Inspector Templeton asked.

Ruby's cheeks flushed. "It's a fashion accessory. Do you like it?"

"You never wear scarves. And you've been fiddling with it since you came in here. You said you visited Jenny at her home. What went wrong?"

I patted his arm. "A small trifle of trouble."

Inspector Templeton's gaze narrowed. "Define small trifle."

"Jenny got angry when Ruby was indelicate about revealing we knew of her condition," I said.

"She didn't hurt you, did she?" Sergeant Matthers asked.

"Jenny choked me for thirty seconds at most," Ruby said. "Her mother came out with a rolling pin and calmed the situation before anything got broken."

Inspector Templeton groaned and sank into his bed. "If these injuries don't kill me, you two will. What were you thinking?"

"We didn't know Jenny was pregnant until we saw her at the farm," I said. "We had to know if Arthur abandoned her when he learned he was to become a father. That would have given her an excellent motive for murdering him."

"When I spoke to Jenny about their relationship, she said it ended weeks ago," Sergeant Matthers said. "There was no bad blood between them."

"You only have her word for that," I said.

Sergeant Matthers shook his head. "I asked around, and everybody said the same. There were no problems between Arthur and Jenny. They parted on friendly terms."

"From everything Jenny's mother said, they were content with the situation and didn't want Arthur in their lives," Ruby said. "She even called him a useless man."

"So many are," I murmured. "We need to go back to the start. We've missed something. I'm still convinced Stanley is innocent. Sergeant Matthers, what about Arthur's brother? Does Ernie's alibi hold water?"

"It's been confirmed. I spoke to a waitress at the officer's club he dined at on the night Arthur died."

"He stayed at the club so late?" I asked.

"It stays open until two o'clock in the morning. He had a late dinner around ten p.m., stayed talking to friends until gone midnight, and then sat drinking whiskey and smoking a cigar. He couldn't have killed Arthur."

"That's unfortunate," I said. "He had an excellent motive. If it's not Ernie or Jenny, it must be Finn. Have you found out where he's hiding?"

"Veronica! Stop pestering Sergeant Matthers. This isn't the only case he's working on," Inspector Templeton said.

"It's all right, sir," Sergeant Matthers said. "We've not found Finn yet. He always vanishes when he gets raided. It happens several times a year. He disappears for a few weeks, then finds a new venue, and off we go again."

"We must winkle him out," I said. "He's behind this. We'll find him, get a confession, and Stanley will be a free man."

Sergeant Matthers gripped his hands in front of him. "I'm sorry to say, but I think it was Stanley. He's been giving us the runaround with his mother's address, so we can't check he was visiting her at the time Arthur was killed."

"Why would he do that?" Ruby asked.

"He's provided us with several wrong addresses. We visited three places, but no one knew her, and she'd never lived in any of the dwellings."

"Stanley did say he didn't want her to be bothered." A squelch of unease curdled my stomach.

"There's good reason for that," Sergeant Matthers said. "It turns out his mother's been dead for two years."

My eyebrows lifted. "Oh! That's unfortunate."

"More than unfortunate," Inspector Templeton said. "It proves he lied."

"We kept pushing Stanley and asking why he wasn't being truthful, but all he would say was he had a bad memory," Sergeant Matthers said. "But you don't forget where your mother lives. I did some digging after the third address proved false, and that was when I found her death record."

"Perhaps he was visiting her grave." The sense of unease intensified. This was serious. Why would Stanley provide a fake alibi if he wasn't involved in Arthur's death?

"He's hiding something, that's for sure," Sergeant Matthers said. "When I told him I knew about his mother being dead, he refused to say anything else."

"Because he's guilty," Inspector Templeton said. "We have our man. The case is closed."

"There must be another reason Stanley provided a false alibi," I said. "Perhaps he was up to no good and is worried he'll lose his job if I find out."

"Or he murdered Arthur and is covering it up," Inspector Templeton said. "Just because he works for you doesn't make him a good person."

"I only employ excellent people," I said. "Even though Stanley hasn't been truthful, I'm not abandoning hope. We've missed a clue or a suspect. Sergeant Matthers, you focus on finding Finn. Once you've located him, arrest him and make sure he doesn't sneak away. Ruby, we'll return to the scene of the crime and see what's been overlooked."

Sergeant Matthers stared at me with wide eyes and then looked at Inspector Templeton, his mouth hanging slightly open.

DEATH AT THE DRIPPING TAP   179

Inspector Templeton sighed and shook his head. "Get used to it, Sergeant. These ladies never give up."

Ruby stopped her car outside the Dripping Tap. It was getting late, almost nine o'clock. I couldn't afford to be out too late, since I didn't want to alarm Matthew again, and our mother would be champing at the bit for the latest news on Arthur's murder.

"It looks busy," Ruby said.

"It's the end of the working week, so people will be spending their hard-earned money. We won't be long. I've known Martha for years, so if she has useful information about Stanley, she'll help." Martha Peabody had worked at the Dripping Tap for over ten years. She was hard working, had a laugh like a coughing drain, and was loyal to the family.

We stepped out of the car and walked the short distance to the pub's entrance. Two rowdy men fell out of the door, laughing together. We stepped back to let them pass, the heady scent of cigarettes and beer drifting out to greet us.

I entered first and was surprised to see there wasn't a spare seat to be had. A man was playing a rowdy number on the piano at the back of the bar, and he had a dozen people singing along to his rousing tune.

We pushed through the crowd of mainly men, getting a number of appraising looks as we passed. We finally made it to the bar, and I waved at Martha to get her attention. She was a sturdy forty-something, with a fashionably short bob and a liking for lashings of dark eyeliner.

"Miss Vale! I've never seen you here on a Friday night." Martha nodded at Ruby.

"I see you're busy, so I won't keep you long," I said.

"Don't mind this lot. They can wait a moment for their beer. What can I get you?"

"Nothing to drink. But I have questions about Stanley."

"Doesn't everyone? I just about fell off my seat when I learned he'd been taken in by the old bill." She pulled a pint for a customer as she talked.

"The situation has got complicated," I said. "We've been trying to figure out what happened, but keep meeting dead ends. I must ensure the wrong man isn't charged with this crime."

"It's good you're helping. He'd never tell you himself, but he likes you."

"He does?"

"Of course! He finds it queer he's got a lady as his boss, but I keep telling him these are modern times and ladies are very capable. We proved that during the war." Martha poured a glass of wine and handed it to a customer before taking their money.

"Indeed we did," I said. "I'm glad to hear Stanley's content in his work."

"He won't be content at the moment. Poor bugger, stuck behind bars and everyone thinking he killed a man. It's a shame. Stanley could be grumpy, but he runs a tight ship. The punters are missing him." She rang up another sale. "What questions have you got?"

"Stanley wasn't truthful about where he was on the night of the murder," I said.

"Ha! What did he tell the police? Suppose he thought he was being clever, giving them the runaround. That went wrong, didn't it."

"Stanley said he was visiting his mother. A mother who's been dead for two years."

Martha pressed her lips together as she served another pint of beer. She wiped her hands on her apron, then marched over and leaned in close. "You didn't hear this from me, but he uses that as a cover."

"Cover for what?" I asked.

Martha glanced over her shoulder, waving away customers' demands. "Stanley likes to fight. That night, he mentioned he had a match arranged. No big deal, but if anyone asked what he was doing, he was visiting his old mother."

"You're talking about bare-knuckle fighting?" Ruby whispered.

"Shush. Of course. It's all the rage around here. I think the men get involved to deal with their frustrations. Many of them served, and now they're back to day-to-day life and finding it dull. I reckon that's why all these underground clubs are springing up. And, of course, when he wins, he makes a nice little earner."

Several of the men waiting to be served started thumping their empty glasses on the bar.

"Keep your hair on. I'm talking to these nice ladies," Martha yelled. "I should get on. Don't want this lot to get too rowdy."

"Thank you." I leaned against the bar. "You've been most helpful."

"Come back when it's quieter, and we can have a drink together." Martha dashed away.

Ruby turned to me, sympathy in her eyes. "If Stanley was involved in these bare-knuckle fights…"

I sighed. "Then it's likely they fought in the ring and trouble brewed between them."

"Stanley got payback on his own terms."

A headache bloomed behind my eyes, and my stomach sank. "With this information, we must confront Stanley." I didn't want him to be guilty, but all the evidence suggested he was.

Chapter 18

I lifted a spoonful of porridge to my mouth, then set it back in the bowl and stirred my breakfast.

"Is it too hot?" Matthew sat on the other side of my mother's bed, eating his own steaming bowl of porridge with gusto.

"It's perfect, as usual. Thank you. I have had no appetite since learning about Stanley's deceit. All this time he's been working for us and I had no idea he was involved in illegal fights."

My mother was sitting up in bed, a breakfast tray placed over her legs as we ate together, and I updated them about the investigation. "I'm worried about the pub's reputation. It's not the nicest area, but this murder could ruin us."

"And of course, a man is dead," I said.

She flapped a hand in the air. "That too! Don't make me out to be a heartless beast. Perhaps it's time we sold the Dripping Tap. Focus on the more pleasant areas."

"Father would have hated that idea," I said. "He knew a respectable pub in a rundown area helped communities. Pubs bring people together. It gives everybody a focus.

If we sold the Dripping Tap, it would be to the area's detriment."

"Your father put too much stock in how important pubs were," my mother said. "And it worries me, you poking about in this business. I don't want you back in the East End."

If she knew half of what Ruby and I had been getting up to during this investigation, it would put her in the hospital for a month. "Perhaps we don't pay Stanley enough. He earns money when he wins a fight. Have we been remiss with wage increases?"

"Your father was one of the most generous employers around," my mother said. "He gave Christmas bonuses and extra holidays. He was never tightfisted, and you're the same. This has got nothing to do with how much we pay Stanley, and more to do with him being a bad egg."

"Do the police really think he's guilty?" Matthew asked.

"I'm afraid they do. And with the new information we uncovered after speaking to Martha at the pub, I think we have the last nail in his coffin."

"Have you told Inspector Templeton yet?" my mother asked.

"No, it was late by the time I got back from the Dripping Tap, and I didn't want to disturb him."

"You should have telephoned the police station directly. Told them the news, had Stanley charged, and this business would be put to bed," my mother said.

"I'm still unsure he's guilty," I said. "Stanley has a murky past, but he does a sterling job for us."

"He's a violent man who lied to the police!"

"His hobby of bare-knuckle fighting isn't to everyone's taste, but something about this case feels wrong."

"Don't tell the police you've got a feeling about this investigation. They'll think your emotions have got the better of you," my mother said. "Leave this to the experts, and you look around for a new landlord for the Dripping Tap. Or better yet, sell the place."

"It's too early to take those steps," I said. "Although I wondered about Martha. She's been there a long time and is more than capable. When the position became vacant, she was looking after a sick relative, so didn't want the extra responsibility. Perhaps things have changed."

"Should a woman be in charge of that pub? It's such a rough area," my mother said.

"You should visit the Dripping Tap. It's very popular, and Martha had everything under control when I was there last night."

"I can't go all that way! But I have been thinking…"

"About what?"

"I'd like to visit Inspector Templeton while he's in the hospital," she said. "Matthew will come with me."

Matthew went pale but nodded. They'd clearly been discussing this matter. I masked my surprise. Mother last left the house to visit the dogs' home to hand over two adorable pugs she'd fostered. Since then, she'd not mentioned a desire to leave her bed, let alone venture out into the world.

"Inspector Templeton would welcome the company. He hates being stuck in bed," I said.

"I only said I'd think about going." Matthew shuffled about and tugged at a sock.

"If you leave the house, you'll need to spend time removing all that puppy fur from those trousers." I gestured at Matthew's typically lived in look.

He shrugged, never one to care about his appearance. "Felix is moulting. I've been brushing him every day, but when he moves, a cloud of fur drifts off him."

"Would you like me to make the arrangements for a visit?" I asked.

My mother finished her porridge. "Not yet. I need to find a time when my heart's not racing like one of Ruby's horses."

I held in a sigh. She often had these grand ideas, but they came to nothing. "You'd brighten his day. Take his mind off of being confined to bed."

"I know how that feels," my mother said.

"Of course you do. I need to go to work. Uncle Harry will have forgotten what I look like if I don't put in an appearance." I happily left Matthew tidying the breakfast things and exited the house with Benji. I decided to walk to work to give myself time to think. I'd barely slept last night. After speaking to Martha and learning about Stanley's underhand dealings, my mind was in a whirl. I should tell the police, but this information only damned Stanley.

Was he guilty?

Perhaps he'd come to blows with Arthur that night. They tussled, things got out of control, and a wild punch was thrown. But both men fought regularly, so they knew their own strength and how to hit without causing permanent damage.

That knowledge led me to one unsettling conclusion. If Arthur and Stanley had come to blows, then Stanley meant to kill Arthur. There was nothing accidental about this death.

I reached the newspaper office, walked in, and everyone cheered.

"It's our criminal free from her cell," someone rudely hollered.

I looked around in startled surprise. Everyone was clapping and whooping.

Our regular tea lady, Doris, walked over with a cake in her hands. Iced on the top, it said *happy release day.*

She shook her head. "This wasn't my idea. And be careful. These idiots insisted a file was baked inside, so it isn't edible. Waste of good cake, if you ask me."

I took the cake, an amused smile on my face. "I'm not sure what to say. Thank you? I'm happy to be a free woman. And prison really wasn't all that taxing."

There was more hollering and clapping.

Uncle Harry strode out of his office. "Enough of that. You've had your fun. Everybody get back to work."

I set the cake on my desk and shrugged off my coat before settling Benji in his usual place.

Bob skulked over, a sour look on his face. "Getting yourself in trouble again?"

"Nothing I can't handle," I said.

"I've had to cover for you."

"Marvellous. Did you write all the obituaries? The pile of work still looks unseasonably large."

"I've been answering the telephone. People have been asking for you."

"My journalistic abilities are in high demand," I said. "You should take a leaf out of my book, and people would be calling to speak to you, too."

"And get myself in trouble with the police, you mean? I'm too smart for that."

"Have you had your IQ tested recently?"

"Enough bickering, you two," Uncle Harry said. "You've both got work to do."

Bob glowered at me before slouching away and returning to his desk.

"Thank you for giving me the extra time off," I said to Uncle Harry.

"Did it help?"

"It uncovered worrying information. If you have a moment, I'd like to talk to you about it."

"Let's go into my office, where we won't be disturbed."

I settled into a chair in Uncle Harry's office, the door closed behind me. "I learned Stanley's been involved in bare-knuckle fights. I don't know for certain, but it's likely he faced Arthur in a match."

Uncle Harry grimaced. "That would be unfortunate. What do the police think?"

"I only found out the news last night, so I've yet to tell them," I said. "I don't want it to be Stanley, but it looks bad for him."

"It does. Have you spoken to Stanley about this new information you've discovered?"

"No, and I wondered if you could put in a good word for me at the police station. I'd like to speak to him on my own, get to the bottom of this. He's been caught out in a lie. His alibi is also false. I'm struggling to find an innocent path for him."

"I can get you an interview," Uncle Harry said. "It'll take me a while, and I'll need to make some calls."

"It would be wonderful if you could help."

"There's a pile of work on your desk. Get started on that, and I'll see what I can do."

I hopped up and kissed him on the cheek before hurrying back to my desk. I was certain if I could see Stanley eye to eye again, I'd know one way or the other if he was guilty.

It was almost lunchtime when Uncle Harry emerged from his office. I'd completed six obituaries and was outlining another involving an overweight vicar and a pork pie that had got lodged in his throat. The pork pie won.

"Let's take a walk," Uncle Harry said as he passed my desk.

I was grateful for the break. I'd forced myself to focus on work and not think about Stanley, but it had been a mental battle.

Once we were outside, Uncle Harry strode around the back of the building to his car.

I followed with Benji. "I thought we were walking."

"It's a long march to the police station. I've secured us a short meeting with Stanley. We're going together."

"I appreciate you getting involved," I said. "He's more likely to talk with you there."

We climbed into the car and merged into the busy London traffic.

"I've been hearing too many worrying things about what you and Ruby have been getting up to while trying to solve this case," Uncle Harry said. "Without Inspector Templeton's steadying gaze, you've become reckless."

"I assure you, his steadying gaze doesn't influence my behaviour one jot."

"This is the first time you've been arrested. And the first time you've come to the attention of a nasty criminal working out of the East End. I also heard from Inspector Templeton that Ruby was choked by a suspect."

"Men are such gossips," I said.

"Is any of this true?"

"Partially. Although not the part about Inspector Templeton having an influence over me," I said. Benji rested his head on my shoulder and softly whined in my ear. "Perhaps we have been rather spirited. I like to think everyone has a decent side and wants to do the right thing, but I've met people during this investigation who have me questioning that belief."

Uncle Harry navigated around a packed open-top bus. "In our line of work, it's easy to become jaded. We always hear the bad news stories and the troubles people face. I like that you still believe everyone has goodness in them. And I don't think you're wrong, but I think you're naïve when you go into some situations. When murder is involved, someone will have a dark heart."

I stared out of the window in silence for several minutes. "Perhaps I've got this all wrong. Stanley is guilty. I misjudged him."

"It's not looking good for him," Uncle Harry said, his tone softer.

"The fact he's refusing to confess is a positive sign," I said. "Even with his back against the wall, he's determined not to give up."

"Is that innocence or stubbornness at work?"

I was unsure, and we continued the rest of the journey in silence, while I mulled over the increasing possibility that Stanley was about to be convicted of murder.

We arrived at the police station. Rather than going through the front door, Uncle Harry led me and Benji around the back. He tapped three times on a door, and an unfamiliar police officer opened it. He looked around and gestured inside. Uncle Harry passed him some money.

"You've got five minutes. Any longer, and someone will notice there's a problem," the officer said.

"Thanks, Ivan. How's the wife?" Uncle Harry gestured for me to follow him as the officer led us along the corridor.

"Just about to give birth. She's barely sleeping, so neither am I."

"Make sure you get her something nice. And keep her off her feet. I remember when my girls were born. My wife had swollen ankles that troubled her something terrible."

"I always look after my girl." Ivan opened a door to reveal Stanley sitting at a table. He looked surprised when he saw us, and even more so when the officer left us alone.

"I won't beat about the bush," I said as I settled into a seat. "Stanley, you've been lying to the police and to me. You gave them a fake alibi for where you were at the time of Arthur's death, and you've been keeping from me that you're involved in bare-knuckle fights to earn extra money. Do you have anything to say for yourself?"

Stanley opened his mouth and then snapped it shut. He looked down, and Benji wandered over and rested his head on Stanley's knee. Stanley spent a moment stroking Benji, seeming not to have the courage to speak.

"I'm disappointed in you," I said. "If you are having money troubles, you should have come to me."

"Ask a woman for money." He snorted his disapproval. "That'll never happen."

"I'm very capable of helping. Are you having money problems?"

"No! You pay a fair wage. It's ... it's not that." Stanley blew out a shaky breath.

"You fight for fun?"

"Easy, Veronica," Uncle Harry cautioned. "Stanley, we need the truth. Time is running out for you. The police are on the verge of charging you with Arthur's murder."

He heaved out a sigh, his hand still resting on Benji's head. "I'm sorry for not being honest. I do fight, and I get paid when I win."

"Have you and Arthur ever been in a match together?" I asked.

"Yes. Three weeks ago. And I lost to him."

"So you wanted revenge?" My heart sank.

"No! I took part in the fights because I needed extra money. But not for myself. I know this looks bad, but I can control my temper. I didn't kill Arthur."

"What did you need the extra money for?" Uncle Harry asked.

"My niece is sick. She's got a weak chest, and living in London does her no good. I've been saving to take the family away to the seaside. Fresh air, that's what she needs."

"That's decent of you." Since Stanley had lied to me before, I wasn't sure I believed him, but it would be a simple task to investigate his extended family. "Why conceal where you were on the night of Arthur's murder?"

"I couldn't take the risk of telling the police and getting Finn's operation shut down. He'd come for me. And when you get on the wrong side of that man, you're done for."

"You were protecting yourself?" I asked.

"I figured the police would have found the killer by now, so I wouldn't need to tell the truth," Stanley said. "But I'm the only one they're interested in. That detective has it in for me. Stuck up jerk."

It was an accurate description of Detective Chief Inspector Taylor. "I'm still looking into things. I've not given up on you."

"Maybe you should. I'm done for. I lost a fight to Arthur, and then a few weeks later, he's found dead outside the pub I manage. I may as well hold my hands up and say I did it. But I promise you, I didn't."

There was a knock on the door, and Ivan looked in on us. "Time is up."

Stanley stood and brushed Benji's fur off his hands.

I caught hold of Stanley's arm as he walked past me. "I'm still fighting in your corner. We will come through this."

"Thanks, Miss Vale. One way or the other, we absolutely will." He left with Ivan.

Uncle Harry sighed as he crossed his arms over his chest. "I'm still not sure about him."

I hesitated, my gaze on the door. "Neither am I."

"You need to tell the police what you've learned," Uncle Harry said. "It's only a matter of time before they figure it out."

I nodded. "Give me one more day before I reveal everything to them."

I didn't know how I'd solve this mystery. All seemed lost, and the answer was out of reach. But if there was one thing I was known for, it was my stubborn-headed determination. And if that didn't help me out of this bind and clear Stanley's name, nothing would.

Chapter 19

My feet felt as if they were encased in concrete boots, weariness in every step as I shrugged on my coat and struggled with this wretched problem. I was having serious doubts about my sleuthing abilities. Did I not know what I was doing? I'd always considered myself an excellent judge of character, but Stanley appeared guilty. Every new clue we unearthed or suspect we spoke to brought us back to him.

"It's most frustrating," I muttered to myself as I stepped onto the pavement.

Benji leaned against my leg and looked up at me, his tail wagging.

"Not you. You're always a good boy and never a frustration. I just wish you could help me winkle out the final clue to solve this puzzle."

He took a few steps in the direction of his favourite park, and I followed. A fast-paced walk may shake away the shadows of doubt surrounding me. I didn't want to admit defeat. And I certainly didn't want to admit I was wrong about Stanley. He was far from perfect, but then who was? Certainly not me. Definitely not Inspector Templeton. Or Ruby. Or my mother.

Somehow, the final piece of this puzzle had been concealed where I couldn't find it.

The wind was hearty and brisk, and I flipped my coat collar to avoid getting a cold neck. I was glad Benji was leading us away from the hustle and bustle of urban life. I wasn't in the mood for gaiety as people jostled towards a fun evening out with friends. What did they have to smile about? A man was about to be charged with murder, and I wasn't sure he'd done it.

Or was I? I could occasionally be too stubborn for my own good. Was this one such occasion?

Benji was trotting ahead of me, but his pace slowed. He occasionally glanced over his shoulder, not looking at me, but behind me.

I turned to see what had caught his attention, but there was nothing out of the ordinary. A few people were striding along, and a lady pushed a baby in a pram. Maybe it was the child's crying he didn't like. The wail was high-pitched. We continued on, but something clearly unsettled him.

One thing I never did was ignore Benji when his attention had been caught. He was a whip-smart dog with an uncanny knack for knowing when trouble approached.

I continued on, moving at a slower pace, pretending to search for something in my handbag. While I did so, I kept glancing out of the corner of my eye to see what was going on behind me. That was when I caught the stealthy movement of someone ducking from shadow to shadow, hoping they wouldn't be noticed.

Someone was following us.

I called Benji to my side, and we continued into the park. It was less busy here, so it would be easy to confront whoever it was. Although Benji was alert, he wasn't anxious, so neither was I. There were no growls or raised hackles, suggesting he wasn't concerned about whoever was tailing us.

We rounded a corner, and I sprinted behind a thicket of bushes, Benji on my heel. I crouched and waited to see who would pass. At first, there was silence. Then hurried footsteps dashed in our direction. I rested a hand on Benji's head so he wouldn't growl and give us away. The footsteps grew closer, matching my rapid heartbeat. At the last second, when they were almost on top of us, I leapt out.

The young man yelped and stumbled back, almost falling. If I hadn't grabbed him by his arm, he would have toppled over.

"Oh! It's you."

Jenny's younger brother, Gregory, stared at me with wide eyes, his breath rasping out of him. "Why were you hiding behind that bush?"

"Because you were stalking me." I kept a tight grip on his arm, but he made no move to flee.

"No! I was following you. I ... I wanted to talk to you. I just didn't know how."

"Talk? How did you know where I worked?" I asked.

"Jenny told me. And I heard her say you were a writer at a newspaper."

"Yes, that's correct. Cleverly worked out." I didn't let go of his arm. "Are you here alone?"

He nodded eagerly. "I thought we could see the rabbits. I miss mine. You have some at your charity."

"There are rabbits at the dogs' home," I said. "Does your family know you're here?"

His bottom lip jutted out. "I can do things on my own. They don't think I can, but I'm clever. I got two buses to come here, and I didn't get lost once."

"That's impressive," I said. "They'll be worried about you, though. Did you leave a note to tell them about your adventure?"

"Jenny won't be bothered. She can be mean. I don't like her anymore."

"Perhaps we could go back to the office and I could telephone her, or your mother. Make sure they know you're safe."

He wrapped his arms around himself and rocked back and forth on his heels. "No! I don't want to go back. You can't make me. I want to see the rabbits."

Benji hurried over and jumped up, resting his paws flat against Gregory's chest. The young man stopped rocking and stared at Benji. Benji licked Gregory's chin, making him laugh. "I like your dog. I like rabbits more, but dogs are nice, too. Rabbits are the best, though. Jenny once said she'd put my rabbit in a pie if I didn't sweep the whole house on my own."

"That wasn't nice," I said. "I can tell you love rabbits."

"I do. Can we go and see them?"

"You want to go now?" I checked my watch. "Aren't you hungry? It's almost dinner time."

"I have apples. You can have one." He fumbled in his pockets and pulled out a small, bruised apple.

"You save that for your journey home," I said. What should I do? Send a poor fellow back after he'd come all this way on such an adventure? I had said I'd show

Gregory the rabbits, but I hadn't expected him to show up so unexpectedly.

He sensed I was unsure. "Please. I won't make any trouble. I know I'm a burden, but I do my best."

"I can well believe that. Don't listen to your big sister if she tells you you're a burden. Siblings can be mean to each other. You should hear the things I say to my brother."

"Do you tell him his rabbits are silly?"

"No, Matthew doesn't have any rabbits, but he does have a puppy with a lame leg. He dotes on that creature almost as much as I do Benji."

"Dote?"

"Yes! Adore. Love. That sort of thing."

He beamed at me. "I dote on rabbits. I wait outside for hours every day, hoping mine will come back, but they never do. I think they've run away. Maybe they don't like me anymore. Jenny said they'd be back, but I can't find them anywhere."

I couldn't stand to see the sad look on his face for a second longer. With determined resolution, I caught hold of his arm and marched us back to the street. "Let's see some rabbits, shall we?"

Half an hour later, a taxi deposited us outside the dogs' home. Gregory stared up at the building with wide eyes as he bounced on his toes. "Is this place full of rabbits?"

"Mostly dogs and a few cats. We have rabbits, too, though. We never turn away an animal if we have room."

"I'll take them all," he said. "We have room for dozens of rabbits at the farm."

"I think your mother may have something to say about that. Let's go in and make some new friends." We walked through the doorway, and I greeted Molly at the reception desk, and let her know we were heading to see the unwanted rabbits.

The small animal pens were in the back of the building, away from the barking and general chaos the dogs caused.

Gregory remained silent, his hand clutching my elbow. He seemed scared, but I think he was just overwhelmed and excited. Benji stuck close to him, now and again wagging his tail or licking the young man's hand to reassure him. He was excellent at picking up when a person felt uneasy and worked hard to make them content.

"Here we are," I said. "We have volunteers who look after the rabbits, along with the rest of the animals. They should have finished the evening rounds, so the rabbits will have already tucked into their dinner and be ready for a rest."

Gregory nodded, his lips pressed together, excited anticipation in his eyes.

"You must be quiet," I cautioned. "You don't want to startle them."

"I'm always careful with rabbits," he whispered. "I want to make sure they like me. I'll dote on them."

"I've no doubt about that." I opened a door that led into a long, thin corridor. There were a dozen cages set aside for the smaller animals we took in. Rabbits and guinea pigs, mainly.

After a quick inspection of each pen, we found three rabbits. One was a large brown floppy-eared creature.

Another was snow white, and the final one was mottled brown.

"This one looks like Floppy." Gregory was crouched in front of a pen, a huge smile on his face. "She was my favourite. I used to sneak her extra carrots. She let me cuddle her."

"She sounds like a sweet rabbit," I said. "If you have spare time, we're always looking for volunteers to help here. If your mother permits it, you'd be welcome to get involved. We even sometimes set up pens in volunteers' gardens if they have the room. You could look after some of the rabbits brought in when we don't have the space to care for them."

His eyes grew even wider, then he shot up and engulfed me in an enormous hug. "I'll be your best friend if you let me do that. I'll take such good care of them."

I laughed. "I can see how fond you are of these creatures. And you'd be helping us out."

Gregory huffed a hot breath in my ear and stepped away, his happiness gone. "Jenny says I'm no good for anything. She won't allow it."

"We'll convince her how wrong she is," I said. "Benji clearly adores you, and none of the rabbits appear scared of you. If animals love you, it shows good character. They're never wrong about a person."

His smile returned. "I could convince Ma to take in some rabbits for me to keep. I mean, for me to look after. For a long time. Maybe forever."

"I can see how happy that would make you," I said. "We'll figure out a plan together. You'll soon have so many rabbits you won't know what to do with yourself."

"Can I hold this one?" Gregory pointed at the snow-white rabbit.

I checked the description we had pinned next to the cage. Every animal who came to the dogs' home was given a behavioural assessment and, when possible, their history recorded so we knew what challenges we'd be dealing with.

"She was given up because the children got bored with her, so she was a family pet, and must be used to being handled. Let me go in and test the water. Then you can have a cuddle." I stepped into the pen and enticed the rabbit out with a lettuce leaf. When she'd finished eating, I carefully scooped her up, being sure to support her powerful back legs, so I didn't get kicked, and held her. She made no objection.

"She likes it!" Gregory twitched with nervy excitement.

"You can come in," I said. "Benji, you wait out there. You don't want to startle the rabbit."

Benji wagged his tail and settled on the floor, watching with interest.

I passed the rabbit to Gregory and gave them a moment to get acquainted. A tear trickled down his cheek as he snuggled her against his chest.

"What's the matter? Don't you like her?" I asked.

"I miss my rabbit," Gregory whispered. "Jenny said I had to help her, and when I said no, she took her. I told you she was mean."

"Oh dear. Were you refusing to do your tasks at the farm?"

He shook his head. "I shouldn't say. It's a secret." He gently stroked the rabbit, sending up plumes of white fur.

"I'm excellent at keeping secrets. Don't you want to share yours with me?"

"I shouldn't. Jenny will get mad with me. She'll shout again."

"Jenny has a temper? Does she ever scare you?"

He nodded glumly. "She's so bossy."

"I'm sure my brother thinks I'm bossy, too," I said. "He's even told me a time or two that I'm too opinionated."

"Is that bad?"

"I think it's excellent to have opinions, but not everyone agrees with me." I watched him pet the rabbit in silence. "Did Jenny ever talk to you about a man she was friendly with? Arthur Blackstone?"

Gregory looked away.

"I was wondering if you ever saw them argue?" I asked.

"I stayed out of it. She told me to, so that's what I did." He gulped and hid his face in the rabbit's fur. "I don't want to talk about it. It makes me sad. Almost as sad as when I realised my rabbit wasn't coming back."

I leaned closer and gently stroked the rabbit's soft fur. A large clump of fur floated down and settled on my skirt. I plucked it off and stared at it, then gasped.

Gregory looked up at me. "What's wrong? Did she bite you?"

I rubbed the fur between my fingers. Suddenly, everything made sense. And suddenly, I felt very uncertain about this young man's future.

Chapter 20

"I'm usually excited when you suggest an adventure," Ruby whispered as she crouched beside me behind a wall close to the farmhouse Jenny and her family lived in. "But this feels unsafe. We've seen how effective Jenny is when she throws a punch."

"Which is why we're keeping concealed," I murmured.

It was barely dawn the next morning, and after spending time with Jenny's brother at the dogs' home yesterday, I'd come to one settled conclusion about who killed Arthur.

"Are you sure you can trust Gregory?" Ruby wrapped an arm around Benji, no doubt feeling the chill as much as I did.

"He's an honest young man," I said. "And he's been dragged into this terrible business against his will. I couldn't convince him to tell me everything, but he promised if I found his missing rabbits, he'd reveal the truth about what he did."

"What if... What if something bad happened to his rabbits?" Ruby asked. "He won't tell you anything then, and this will all be for nothing."

"Jenny took those rabbits because she knew how much they meant to Gregory. He'd do anything to get them back."

Ruby was silent for a few seconds. "Even murder?"

"He's hiding a huge secret. And he's a big lad. Strong, too."

"He seemed sweet when we spoke to him about his rabbits," Ruby said.

"I'd kill for Benji."

"You would not!"

I tickled Benji under the chin. "Let's hope I never have to test that promise."

Ruby sighed. "I hope the police have telephoned by now."

"Sergeant Matthers promised he would."

"What's taking so long?" Ruby jiggled on the spot. "If they don't leave soon, I'll need to find a rather large bush to duck behind."

"It's your own fault. You drank too much tea this morning."

"I needed something to wake me up. After your telephone call last night telling me what you had planned, I barely slept a wink."

"This will all be over soon, and life can go back to normal."

"For a brief few moments until you find a new case to get stuck into," Ruby said. "Not that I'm complaining. You make my life jolly interesting. Although next time, let's lurk somewhere warmer and with better facilities."

I tensed as the farmhouse door opened. There were muffled voices, but I couldn't see anyone.

"Jenny had better not spot us hiding here," Ruby whispered.

"She'll be too concerned about what the police want with her and Gregory to notice us," I said.

Gregory tumbled out of the door, and Jenny appeared a few seconds later. She shoved him in the shoulder, and they headed towards a beaten-up looking van.

"Jenny terrifies Gregory," I whispered. "He was crying when he spoke about her."

"I can see why. She's a terrible bully. I know you sometimes tease Matthew, but this sibling relationship is very different. It's not healthy."

We waited another few moments until the van was out of sight before creeping from our hiding place.

"We must be careful," I whispered. "Mrs Crawshaw is still at home. We don't want to get caught looking for the rabbits."

"They'll need to be stored in somewhere secure," Ruby said. "Otherwise, they'd have hopped away, and never be seen again."

"Let's start our search inside the barns. And it won't take long, not with our secret weapon on hand." I patted Benji's side.

He wagged his tail, ready to get to work.

I pulled out a small amount of the rabbit fur I'd collected from the dogs' home last night. It wasn't an exact match to the scent we needed to find, but it would give Benji an idea of what we searched for. I let him sniff it for a moment, and then we headed off, Benji's nose to the ground, while I watched the farmhouse for signs of movement.

We stayed behind the house and headed towards the largest of the barns. The door creaked as Ruby pulled it open, and she froze.

"Hurry! The sooner we get inside and out of sight, the better," I whispered. "I suspect the family keeps shotguns. We don't want to be confronted with an angry mother who's defending her land."

"Perish the thought." Ruby slipped through the gap. Benji went next, and I was the last inside, securing the door behind us.

We spent a few minutes looking around the hay-scented barn, each of us heading off in a different direction to cover as much ground as quickly as possible.

Ruby's gasp had me turning. "Have you found something?"

"A collection of unpleasant animal traps," Ruby said. "And they look recently used. I hope Jenny didn't use them on her brother's rabbits."

I grimaced. Cruel animal traps were a countryside practice I couldn't abide. I understood the need to protect local wildlife, but there were kinder methods of deterrent than vicious traps that injured animals and left them to suffer.

Benji softly barked, drawing our attention. We hurried over to find him standing in front of a stack of hay bales.

"The rabbits won't be in there," Ruby said. "Are you sure you've got the right scent, Benji?"

He woofed again and nosed at the hay bales.

I walked around them. They were laid out in a square rather than stacked on top of each other. "Help me to move this one."

Ruby complained as we shifted the heavy bale, straw floating around us, and making me want to sneeze.

"Oh! Will you look at that? They've been here all this time." Ruby smiled at me as we uncovered two cages hidden in the hay bale fort containing three rabbits. One of them was snow white.

"That must be the missing Floppy," I said. "Gregory was very keen on a white rabbit staying at the dogs' home."

"I'm glad they're unharmed," Ruby said. "It would have been heartbreaking to tell the poor young man his beloved pets were no more."

"This is excellent. We have what we need," I said. "We'll give Gregory back his rabbits, and he'll reveal the truth."

"That he murdered Arthur?" Ruby stared at the rabbits as she tugged on her bottom lip.

"It doesn't make me happy, either. We'll have to ensure the police know he was coerced by Jenny. She must be involved. Arthur abandoned her when he learned she was with child, and she made Gregory attack him in revenge. Gregory said Jenny made him do things he didn't want to do."

Ruby crouched and poked a finger through the cage bars. "And murder was one of those things. She said he'd never get his rabbits again unless he did what she told him."

"Unfortunately, that still makes him guilty of a terrible crime." I glanced about. "We need something to put these rabbits in, and then we'll head to the Dripping Tap. By the time we get there, Sergeant Matthers will have rounded up the suspects, and we can put this matter to bed once and for all."

It took us fifteen minutes to find small wooden boxes to put the rabbits in. They were easy to handle, a testament to how kind Gregory was to them, and I was soon settled on the back seat of Ruby's car with Benji, the boxes secured beside me as we whizzed back to the pub.

Given the early hour, the streets were almost deserted, and we made it back in record time, mainly thanks to Ruby and her inability to take her foot off the gas pedal and remember there was a brake.

When we pulled up outside the Dripping Tap, two police officers were stationed outside.

"Sergeant Matthers isn't messing around," Ruby said. "I've been so impressed with him. I'll have to insist Inspector Templeton gives him a promotion."

"He has come good for us," I said. "When I spoke to Sergeant Matthers last night on the telephone, he was startled by my discovery, but happy to help get everyone together so we could solve this murder."

"He's a first-rate police officer." Ruby turned in her seat and looked at the rabbits. "I hope they haven't had any little accidents."

"They may have done. Your driving was particularly terrifying."

She gently snorted. "My driving is excellent."

"You go inside, make sure everybody is there, then give me a sign. I'll bring in the rabbits."

"Righty ho." Ruby hopped out, brushed straw off her clothing, and dashed into the pub. She emerged a moment later and waved at me.

I called over one of the officers and requested assistance with the rabbits, making sure he knew to keep the box secured so nobody escaped at the last moment. I followed him into the pub, carrying one box containing a rabbit, with Benji beside me.

All the suspects were there, including Stanley. He looked surprised and a little careworn, but there was a hopeful glint in his eyes. I nodded at him. My landlord's name would soon be cleared of any wrongdoing.

Jenny stood with Gregory, looking sullen, while Gregory appeared confused. Arthur's older brother, Ernie, was also there, dressed in a smart suit and not looking happy to have his morning routine disturbed. Patrick, the illegal lodger, was also in attendance, looking as if he'd been pulled out of bed and dressed in the dark.

"No sign of Finn?" I murmured to Sergeant Matthers.

"He's long gone. But I've ruled him out as a suspect. He was entertaining a lady friend that evening after the fight, and she vouched for him."

"Well, that's one less problem to deal with." I set down the box I'd carried in and instructed the officer to do the same with his boxes.

"What's this all about?" Jenny asked. "The police demanded we show up here, or they'd bring us in. I've got a business to run. Our mother can't do it on her own. Not with her arthritis."

"It's about murder," I said. "Arthur Blackstone's murder. He was discovered outside this pub after being brutally attacked and left for dead."

"That's got nothing to do with me," Patrick said. "I've got the best alibi."

"You were a suitable suspect, though," I said. "Ruby and I discovered you stealing from Arthur's room. And when my dog caught you, we found Arthur's personal possessions on you. It was a most unpleasant thing to do, stealing from a dead man."

Patrick's cheeks flushed. "Life's been hard on me. Do you think I wanted to sleep on Arthur's floor if I had any other option? And as I told the police, he was dead, so he didn't need his things. Give them to a man who can make use of them."

"It was badly done," I said. "And it would have been easy for the police to assume you killed Arthur so you could take his possessions."

"Desperate men do desperate things," Ruby said.

"But... But my alibi." Patrick gestured at Sergeant Matthers.

"Yes, fortunately for you, the police witnessed you selling, no doubt, stolen goods in a different part of London. It would have been impossible for you to kill Arthur," I said.

Patrick blew out a breath. "At least I'm innocent of something."

I looked at Stanley, and he tensed. "I'm sorry you found yourself in such an unfortunate situation, but you must admit, the police had every right to keep you behind bars while they investigated."

Stanley's forehead furrowed. "I've made a few mistakes."

"You hid useful information that could have solved this crime faster," I said. "And the more that was uncovered, the guiltier you seemed. Your violent past, your involvement in bare-knuckle fighting, and the fact you provided a false alibi made you the obvious prime suspect."

"It sounds like it was him," Jenny said.

"It wasn't," I said. "Stanley has an alibi. He was fighting. Of course, it was hard to find any witnesses because if they admitted to seeing that fight, they'd be revealing their involvement in betting on illegal sports." I looked at Sergeant Matthers.

He nodded. "We found someone willing to confirm what Stanley was up to that night. He couldn't have murdered Arthur."

Stanley sagged against the bar. "I know I messed up, but I did it for the right reason."

"Yes, your desire to obtain extra funds to help your family is admirable. I just wish you'd spoken to me rather than getting involved in something so unpleasant. You'd have saved yourself a heap of trouble and not been detained in a prison cell for such a long time."

He lowered his head. "I'm sorry. I've got a good thing here, and I've messed it all up."

"We'll talk about that another time." I turned my attention to Ernie, whose nose was slightly wrinkled, his displeasure clear at being summoned to such a rough part of town. "When I spoke to you, it was obvious there was no love for Arthur."

"And I make no apologies for that. I was open about the fact we didn't have a relationship. We were born into the same family, but that was our only connection," Ernie said.

"You've made yourself a wonderful life," I said. "Associating with the successful and wealthy. Your heroism during the war has served you well."

"It could have done the same for Arthur, if he'd followed in my footsteps, instead of turning to a life of crime," Ernie said.

"It must have been an embarrassment to have such a disreputable member of your family tainting your unblemished record."

"Now, hold on a moment. I've not spoken to Arthur in over a year," Ernie said. "I cut him out of my life."

"But you had a motive for wanting him dead." Ernie's arrogance irritated me, so I wanted him to squirm. "You're still moving up in the world, and I'm sure you have grand ambitions. You may have decided to remove the stain of disgrace from your name. Arthur's squalid behaviour could have ruined things for you."

"I'd never do something so cowardly." Ernie tugged on his tailored suit sleeves.

"We had to consider you," I said. "Fortunately for you, your alibi was confirmed."

By now, Jenny looked uncomfortable, her gaze shooting around the pub as if seeking an escape route.

"We must also consider the mastermind behind the bare-knuckle fights," I said.

Jenny's expression brightened. "Yes! It was Finn. Those two were always getting into fights."

"Finn would have needed his bare-knuckle fights to stay a secret," I said. "When the police learn of their location, they always shut them down."

"That's right. Finn was worried Arthur would brag about the fights and get us in trouble. My cousin is always one step ahead of the law. Anyone who talks doesn't last for long." She nudged Gregory to get him to agree with her, but he sullenly stared at the floor.

"And Finn's achieved that so far. However, he didn't murder Arthur." I opened one of the boxes and extracted Floppy.

Gregory yelped with delight and dashed away from Jenny to scoop the rabbit out of my arms. He snuggled the creature against his chest, tears in his eyes. "You found her. You said you would, and you did. Floppy is home!"

"She never left. She'd been hidden on the farm," I said. "I suspect, by your sister."

"Why would I hide his bleedin' rabbits?" Jenny glowered at me.

"You took them to force Gregory to commit a terrible deed." I turned to him and rested a hand on his arm. "It was the rabbit fur that provided the final clue to this mystery."

"What fur?" Jenny asked.

"When Arthur's body was found, the police identified what they thought were white wool fibres on his clothing. It wasn't wool. It was white rabbit fur. Fur from Gregory's favourite pet."

Jenny sucked in a breath.

I turned to Gregory. "You murdered Arthur, didn't you?"

Chapter 21

Gregory froze, the rabbit still clutched to his chest. "I didn't do it."

Jenny's face paled, but she remained silent, her fierce gaze on her brother.

"Not willingly, but you did what you had to do, to get back your precious pets," I said. "I understand. I'd do anything to keep Benji safe, but murder is wrong."

Gregory's gaze was frantic as he looked at Jenny. "Tell them it wasn't me."

She chewed on her bottom lip. "I tried to stop him. Gregory doesn't know his own strength. But he's simple. You can't put him away for this crime. He doesn't understand what he did."

The door to the pub slammed open, and Mrs Crawshaw barged in, still in curlers that were hidden under a hairnet, brandishing an enormous rolling pin. "What's going on?"

"Ma! What are you doing here?" Jenny was poised on her toes, her eyes wide with shock.

"I followed them, didn't I." She waved the rolling pin in my direction. "These two hoity-toitys and their dog snooped around the farm after you left. I knew something was up, so when they drove off, I came after them. I didn't expect to be brought here, though."

"My apologies for being at your farm unannounced, but it was a matter of urgent business," I said.

Mrs Crawshaw sniffed. "Will someone tell me what's going on? Or do I need to use this rolling pin to knock sense into the lot of you?"

Sergeant Matthers bravely stepped into the breach. "Your son was about to confess to murdering Arthur Blackstone."

She snorted derisively. "Him! He rescues ladybirds and puts out food for hedgehogs. He wouldn't hurt a flea. He's not got it in him to kill anybody."

"Gregory didn't know what he was doing," Jenny said, a touch of frantic desperation in her tone. "I told him about Arthur, and he got so angry."

"Angry about what? We agreed we were better off without Arthur in our lives. We're raising the baby ourselves, and that's an end to it," Mrs Crawshaw said.

"I understand why you gave Gregory a false alibi for the night of Arthur's murder," I said to her. "You want to protect your child, but he's done something terribly wrong."

Her fingers flexed around the rolling pin. She stared at Jenny and Gregory in silence for several seconds. "It wasn't him."

"Ma! Keep your mouth shut," Jenny said. "Gregory will be fine. They won't charge someone who's not all there. He came out simple and doesn't know what he's doing most of the time."

"Yes, they will," Mrs Crawshaw said. "And you're right, Miss Vale. I always want to protect my children, even when they're adults making mistakes I can't fix."

"Are you admitting you covered for Gregory on the night of the murder?" I asked.

"I covered for both of them," she said after a long pause. "And it's not Gregory you should be looking at. Jenny is always getting him in trouble. But he's a good boy. When Arthur was killed, he cried all night. He ... he told me what happened."

"What are you doing?" Jenny hissed. "Don't you want to see your grandchild when it's born?"

Mrs Crawshaw's gaze settled on Jenny's slightly swollen stomach. "Jenny forced Gregory to help her. He's not got a violent thought in his head. Never has done. But she took those rabbits and threatened to kill them."

"It was Jenny who killed Arthur?" Sergeant Matthers appeared confused, his gaze shooting from Gregory and back to Jenny.

Mrs Crawshaw heaved out a sigh. "Jenny took him with her that night and forced him to hold Gregory so she could hit him. Jenny punches as hard as any man."

"Ma! Stop. I have everything worked out," Jenny said.

"And I've worked out a few things, too," Mrs Crawshaw said. "I may not be as clever as you, but I know a wrong 'un when I see one. And you're it. You enjoy hurting people. You always played too rough with your brother, even though he begged you to stop. And Arthur had had enough of you. I'm embarrassed to say, she laid hands on him. That was the reason they parted."

"Will you be quiet!" Jenny spat out, rage flushing her cheeks and causing her hands to fist.

"I've had enough of keeping your dark secrets, my girl," Mrs Crawshaw said. "Come here, Gregory. We'll look after each other. We don't need the likes of her in our lives. I may have given birth to her, but she's no longer mine."

I was startled and impressed by Mrs Crawshaw's determination to do the right thing. It couldn't be easy to give up one of her children to save the other. It showed remarkable strength of character.

"You were an awful mother. And you've always liked him more than me, even though he's wrong in the head." Jenny's rage grew as she advanced on her family.

Mrs Crawshaw swung the rolling pin.

"That's enough!" Sergeant Matthers and his team got to work escorting Jenny out as she cursed at her family. Gregory was also taken out after handing me Floppy and making me promise I'd look after her.

I held the rabbit and sighed. The case was solved, the killer found, and her accomplice taken in, too. Although now I knew the full story, I wasn't finished with helping that young accomplice quite yet.

"I can manage on my own." Inspector Templeton made a bungling job of moving his wheelchair. "I don't even need to be in this thing. It's embarrassing."

I tucked a blanket over his knees, ignoring his admonishments. Three days had passed since Jenny and Gregory were taken in for Arthur's murder. Not only was that a cause for celebration, but today was the day Inspector Templeton was being released from the hospital. Although, the way he was griping, he didn't seem happy about being given his freedom.

"I've checked your room, and we've got everything." Ruby hurried along the corridor. "And I even had time to flirt with that dashing doctor who discharged you. You should have told me you had such a handsome man looking after you and I'd have visited every day."

"I can't say I noticed." Inspector Templeton grabbed the bag containing his belongings from Ruby and settled it on his lap.

"There'll be no more doctors or nurses for a while." I moved behind the wheelchair and pushed it towards the exit. "It's back home and plenty of bed rest for you."

"We can be his nurses." Ruby chuckled at Inspector Templeton's groaned protest.

"I don't want you to keep looking in on me," Inspector Templeton said. "I've arranged for a lady to help me for two weeks until I'm properly back on my feet."

"I'm thrilled to hear that," I said. "Although I have extra time now Arthur's murder has been solved, so I can drop by most days."

"Please don't." Inspector Templeton frowned at nothing in particular. "That was a good outcome. And solved thanks to a rabbit's fur."

"And a mother who was determined to protect her son," I said.

"You have Rodney, sorry, Sergeant Matthers, to thank for much of that," Ruby said. "He's an absolute smasher. So obliging."

"I know how hard he's been working and how much patience it takes to deal with the two of you," Inspector Templeton said. "I'll be sure to take him for a pint and a pie as a thank you."

"I was thinking he deserved a promotion," Ruby said.

"I'm not sure I can help with that." Inspector Templeton glanced over his shoulder at me. "What's the latest in the case?"

"Jenny has been formally charged with Arthur's murder," I said. "She got angry with the police and started throwing punches. She admitted to what she did."

"And her brother?"

"Gregory is being charged as an accomplice," I said. "I'm fighting in his corner, though and ensuring he gets an appropriate medical assessment. With his diminished capacity, I'd prefer to see him properly looked after, or maybe involved in community activities. I suggested to Sergeant Matthers there was a volunteer role for him at the dogs' home. Gregory could serve a community sentence. Prison is no place for such an innocent."

"Sergeant Matthers will do the best thing for him," Inspector Templeton said. "It's not the first time we've dealt with cases where men with mental disabilities have got themselves in trouble. In the past, they'd be sent to an institution or an asylum and left to rot, but I'm happy to say, times are changing."

"I'm glad to hear it," I said. "Gregory is an excellent fellow. He was just badly guided by his cruel sister."

"Veronica is looking after all of Gregory's rabbits until his sentence is passed," Ruby said. "Felix and Benji are delighted to have new companions in the house."

"And the rabbits' fur is only plaguing my mother's allergies a fraction of what a litter of kittens would do," I said.

"It sounds like you've got everything in hand," Inspector Templeton said. "I suspect Jenny will receive a lighter sentence given her pregnancy. It's not popular to put a pregnant woman behind bars."

"I hope she's properly looked after," I said. "Her mother has expressed an interest in caring for the child when it's born. She's a fierce woman, so she'll get her own way. But if Jenny is ever to see that child, she must reform. She's a bad sort and horribly mistreated Gregory."

I hit a bump, and Inspector Templeton lost his bag, which fell to the floor. I dashed around to pick up the scattered items, lifting an open letter. I couldn't help but see it was from Detective Chief Inspector Taylor.

"Give that to me!" Inspector Templeton grabbed for it, but I kept reading. "Veronica! That is none of your business."

I remained crouched on the floor, my gaze shifting to Inspector Templeton. "You're being discharged from the police force?"

"Whatever for?" Ruby asked. "You're on the mend. The doctor is happy with how your leg is healing."

Inspector Templeton reached for the letter, and I handed it over. "Detective Chief Inspector Taylor has been worried about me. He's been visiting daily and talking to the doctors, demanding to know when I'll be returning to work."

"You are getting better, aren't you?" A shiver of concern tickled my spine.

"I'm healing, but it's slow." Inspector Templeton shoved the letter back into the bag. "Detective Chief Inspector Taylor believes my injuries are too severe. I'm no longer considered fit for duty."

"This is a mistake." I stood and settled my hands on my hips. "The man hasn't understood what the doctors have told him. I've seen you out of bed and moving about. Yes, you're stiff, but such an injury won't heal in a few weeks. It could take months."

"The chief is right." Inspector Templeton gripped the handles of his bag. "I kept hoping the doctor had made a mistake, and he was being cautious about my recovery. But..."

"Oh dear," Ruby said. "Have you not been truthful with us?"

"As I keep telling you both, this is my business to deal with how I see fit," he said. "You fussing around me like a pair of old hens is making me nervous. Besides, I didn't want to worry you. Not when there's nothing you can do to fix this situation."

I discreetly gestured for Ruby to leave.

"I'll fetch the car so we don't have far to push the wheelchair. Be back in a minute." She hurried out of the door.

I moved the wheelchair to one side of the corridor, locked the wheels, and crouched in front of Inspector Templeton, placing a hand on one of his knees. "What did you think I would do when I learned the truth?"

His gaze moved over my head, his eyes shining with anger. "I'm useless and unwanted. My life was my career. I had a plan. I would have made Detective Chief

Inspector in ten years. Now, I'm out of the force. I'm a broken man who can barely walk."

"You're being ridiculous." I kept my tone soft, aware of the knife-edge he teetered upon. Inspector Templeton was a proud man who'd devoted his life to ensuring justice was done and wrong righted. It was one of the many things I admired about him.

"I don't know what to do," he said. "I had a path I was on and it made me happy. Now, there's nothing ahead of me. A stagnant existence, dealing with a damaged leg and sympathy from people who feel obliged to stay in my life."

"You're being maudlin and miserable, and I've indulged it for long enough." I hopped up and pressed a kiss to his cheek. "You're not useless. And you're very much wanted. Wanted by me."

His mouth dropped open, and he looked up at me, his hand lifting to touch his cheek where I'd kissed it.

"Don't appear so shocked. It's rare I entertain the annoyances of a man for such a long period. I like you, Jacob. Yes, you're stubborn, and often get things wrong, but we're an excellent combination. Admittedly, we bicker like a dog and cat, fighting for no obvious reason, but when we stop sparring, we get along famously. Besides, I can't abandon you. My mother adores you."

He choked out a laugh. "I ... I don't know what to say."

"Neither do I. Not really. That speech wasn't planned," I said. "But I refuse to let you dwell on your troubles. Not when you have so much ahead of you. So many adventures to undertake."

"Veronica, although I appreciate these words, you can't solve this for me. The police don't want me."

"But I do."

"To do what? Work in one of your pubs?"

A smile twinkled across my lips. "Oh, no. I have much bigger plans than that for you."

"What plans?" He appeared flabbergasted, most likely from my unexpected kiss, but also from this startling revelation still forming in my head.

"We can talk about all of that. Besides, my excellent landlord, Stanley, who still has a job you'll be happy to hear, gave me the perfect idea."

Inspector Templeton blinked up at me. "What would that be?"

I moved around to the back of the wheelchair, unlocked the wheels, and pushed him to the exit just as Ruby was pulling up outside. "While you recover, we're going to the seaside. I have several pubs in Kent that are long overdue attention, and there are some charming resorts to enjoy. Fresh air, sunshine, and fish and chip suppers. It will be marvellous."

"The seaside! But ... but how?"

"It's perfectly simple. Pack your bags, Ruby has offered to drive, and off we go."

"Your job at the newspaper! Your mother and Matthew?"

"That's all been arranged," I said. "I have some holiday time saved, and after much discussion and an undue amount of fretting, my mother and Matthew will be joining us in Margate. The beaches are rather lovely. And doesn't everybody enjoy the seaside?"

Ruby poked her head out of the car window. "Did somebody say seaside? I have a wonderful two-piece I've been desperate to try out. I'll look super in it. Perhaps I'll find my prince charming among the sandcastles and waves."

I laughed and rested a hand on Inspector Templeton's shoulder. Although I really should start calling him Jacob since I'd kissed him. "I have everything planned. So, what do you say, Inspector? Shall we go on this adventure together?"

Historical notes

Unexploded bombs: Although London in the early 1920s was full of hope and a sense of live-in-the-moment following the end of the war, danger still lurked. German air raids during the Great War (First World War) began in early 1915, when Zeppelins bombed coastal targets in Eastern England. Gotha aircraft bombings began in May 1917 and they made daylight raids on the southeast of England.

Between June 1917 and May 1918, Gotha bombers made seventeen attacks on London and other southeastern towns.

Not all of those bombs exploded, and a number were lost in the rubble. In Death at the Dripping Tap, I wanted to explore what happened to the plucky officers and volunteers who discovered these bombs. Not all the outcomes had happy endings, like Inspector Jacob Templeton's.

London's East End: East London has a troubled history, full of trials for the people who lived there as the area developed. It was a heavily industrialised area, including shipbuilding, dock work, textile production, and manufacturing. This created overcrowded housing, pollution, and poor sanitation.

The work available through industry meant people flocked to the East End looking to earn a wage. Those wages were low, so the opportunity to have a healthy life was limited. Large families would often live in a few rooms, often surrounded by other families. Overcrowding caused diseases to spread quickly.

The poor quality environment and lack of opportunities saw a rise in crime and alcoholism. Criminal gangs evolved, developing rings of illegal activity, including bare knuckle fighting.

Another point of interest is that East London's reputation is interwoven with the Jack the Ripper murders from the late 19th century. He targeted women in the overcrowded, poor areas of Whitechapel.

Fortunately, over time, the area has undergone regeneration and gentrification (although there are still challenges.) Many areas are now vibrant with rich, thriving cultural scenes.

The Dripping Tap: There is no pub called the Dripping Tap in this area, but I based the location on the Old Blind Beggar pub, which opened in 1894, and is a Victorian pub.

The building itself is a classic Victorian design, and the history of this pub is gripping, located on the old Mile End Toll Gate, where Jack the Ripper committed many of his crimes.

In 1904, a member of a group of pickpockets who were well known to locals visited the pub and stabbed a man in the eye during a brawl!

Skip forward to the 1960s, and infamous East End gangster Ronnie Kray, walked into the pub and shot a man dead.

All that gory history provided the perfect location to drop a body and give Veronica a new mystery to solve!

The pub is still open, but is a much happier, benign place, often visited by university students. And unless they're being stealthy, no gangsters or serial killers drink there.

Also by

Death at the Fireside Inn
Death at the Drunken Duck
Death that the Craven Arms
Death at the Dripping Tap
Death at the Harbour Arms

More mysteries coming soon. While you wait, why not investigate the back catalogue of K.E. O'Connor (Kitty's alter ego.)

About the author

Immerse yourself into Kitty Kildare's cleverly woven historical British mysteries. Follow the mystery in the Veronica Vale Investigates series and enjoy the dazzle and delights of 1920s England. Kitty is a not-so-secret pen name of established cozy mystery author K.E. O'Connor, who decided she wanted to time travel rather than cast spells! Enjoy the twists and turns.

Join in the fun and get Kitty's newsletter (and secret wartime files about our sleuthing ladies!)

Newsletter: https://BookHip.com/JJPKDLB
Website: www.kittykildare.com
Facebook: www.facebook.com/kittykildare

Printed in Great Britain
by Amazon